Alan St. Aubyn

To his own master

A Novel. Vol. 1

Alan St. Aubyn

To his own master
A Novel. Vol. 1

ISBN/EAN: 9783337046538

Printed in Europe, USA, Canada, Australia, Japan

Cover: Foto ©Andreas Hilbeck / pixelio.de

More available books at **www.hansebooks.com**

TO HIS OWN MASTER

A Novel

BY

ALAN ST. AUBYN

AUTHOR OF

'A FELLOW OF TRINITY,' 'THE JUNIOR DEAN,' 'THE OLD MAID'S
SWEETHEART,' ETC.

IN THREE VOLUMES
VOL. I.

London

CHATTO & WINDUS, PICCADILLY

1893

CONTENTS OF VOL. I.

TO HIS OWN MASTER

CHAPTER I.

THE CROOKED STICK.

THE Rev. Thomas Banister, M.A., was really a lucky fellow. Providence had been good to him all round.

It would be hard to give a list of the good things that a Kind Hand—let us call it by the right name, not chance or Providence—had heaped upon this young man's head.

It had given him, to begin with, a good father, the Vicar of a West Country parish;

a good mother goes without saying. What man ever did anything in the world, or was worth anything, who hadn't a good mother ?

The paternal living in the sweet West Country was a poor living to be held by a poor man, and Tom Banister's father had no private means ; and he had by way of compensation a large family.

He had no means whatever outside his profession. His one aim in life, besides the duties of his sacred office, which no man ever more conscientiously fulfilled, was to give his sons an education befitting their station.

He had nothing else to give them.

There were five sons in that poor West Country Vicarage, and, one by one, by dint of much self-denial—that seemed to them in after-life, looking back to it across the years, nothing short of heroic—they were sent out from the parent nest equipped for the battle of life.

They knew something even at the time of the daily denial of those gentle, self-less lives, and of the suffering, and pinching, and scraping of those hard, hard times. They knew enough to thank God every day of their lives, when they had grown to be men, for His unspeakable gift—the gift of loving, self-denying parents.

Those who had borne the suffering and privation so willingly were asleep now under the grass in the green churchyard outside the Vicarage gate, where they had lived and suffered.

All the sons who had once gathered round that frugal board were provided for now—well provided for. The truth of the old adage had been proved : the righteous had not been forsaken for a single day, and his seed were certainly not begging their bread.

Tom Banister, the youngest of the five

stalwart sons, was so fortunate as to win a
sizarship at a college in Cambridge, which
we will call St. Botolph's, St. Botolph being
the patron saint of beggars and poor men.
Not that there were many poor men at
St. Botolph's in Tom Banister's time. There
was not an undergraduate among them who
wore such a threadbare coat as poor Tom,
or eked out his slender allowance with such
painful economy and forethought.

Oh, the humiliations and shifts of those
early days !

It touched him, when a man, to look back
on the humiliations of that bare student life,
its hardships and privations ; but it touched
him more deeply to remember that, when the
struggle was over and he reaped the harvest
of those early trials, the generous father
who had often sent him his last shilling,
when appealed to in some pressing need,
was no longer there to see it.

When prosperity came to Tom Banister, it came with a bound. It brought him quite early in his career, when most men are content to be curates, a living—a comfortable living to some men, a rich living to him. Providence did not stop with the living. She had richer gifts in store, and she gave him of her best—her very best. She gave him a lovely wife, and in due course she gave him two lovely children.

What more was there left for him to desire? What more could Providence find to give him?

She had given him the unspeakable gift of Love. With this great gift were the lesser gifts of health and strength, a handsome person, and a manly frame.

Nature had done her best for Tom Banister, and Fortune, in happy emulation, had added her ample store.

There was not a single cloud on his fair

horizon. His cup was quite full—dangerously full—full to the brim.

The living of Thorpe Regis in the West Country was a town living. There was only one church in the town—the parish church.

One church provided ample accommodation for the congregation of St. Michael's, for Dissent had established a firm foothold in Thorpe.

There were already five chapels belonging to different denominations, and any day there might be a sixth. The Christians of Thorpe Regis had a habit of quarrelling among themselves, and breaking up into little factions, and setting up rival conventicles.

Their quarrels had nothing to do with Tom Banister. His congregation never quarrelled. They were quite a happy family.

There were daily services in the parish church; that is, prayers were read every

day, and a sermon was preached on Wednes-
day evenings, and there were early celebra-
tions on Sundays and saints' days. There
were the usual parish clubs and friendly
societies, something going on every day in
the week : Bible - classes, or temperance
meetings, or Young Men's or Young
Women's Associations, or Bands of Hope,
or mothers' meetings. There was always
something to keep a curate's zeal from flag-
ging ; in addition to all these things there
was the school.

It was not a Board school ; it was an old-
fashioned National school, where the Bible
was read and taught in the old-fashioned
way. It wasn't read only ; it was taught,
and the curate had to spend one hour of his
busy day in teaching it. Model-drawing and
perspective and the piano were not in the
curriculum ; the budding agricultural mind
was sufficiently exercised in grasping, in a

feeble, rudimentary way, the three R's, and in stumbling through the Church Catechism.

What with visiting the sick, teaching the children, attending the meetings, and taking the daily services, the work of the curate of St. Michael's was cut out. If he did his duty he would not have a minute to himself all the week.

Tom Banister had been particularly lucky in his curates : it was nothing new for him to be lucky ; it would have been an exception to the rule if anything had gone wrong with him.

He had been so fortunate as to keep one curate four years—an exemplary young man, who had done all, and more than all, he was required to do ; who had never neglected a single duty during all these busy months and years, and had contrived to put in not a few works of supererogation.

He had his reward in due time.

When a vacancy occurred in the living of the adjoining village of Thorpe St. Mary, the Bishop of the diocese offered it to Banister's hard - working curate, and the Rector of Thorpe Regis had to look out for a successor. He promptly advertised in the *Guardian* for a curate. No doubt if the *Guardian* had been in existence in St. Paul's days, he would have made his wants known through that excellent medium, when Barnabas had quarrelled with him and Mark had turned away from the work.

It did not occur to Tom Banister, as it occurs to thin-skinned people in the present day, that it was humiliating to advertise for a curate. He had advertised often enough for a curacy in those old days, and he still recollected the avidity with which he used to read through the list of 'Wanted' in the columns of the *Guardian*.

Other curates read them with avidity now,

and the result of their reading caused his post-bag to overflow for several mornings after his advertisement had appeared.

The answers to this advertisement were a considerable source of trouble to the Rector of St. Michael's.   His correspondents were so full of ' views.'   He hadn't any ' views ' in particular himself, except to do his duty according to his lights, and teach the old-fashioned doctrine of the Church of England.

From among the mass of correspondence he chose a young man who hadn't any ' views,' or, at least, he didn't mention them.

Perhaps he did not choose wisely.

He was hampered all the time with a dreadful suspicion that, according to the old rhyme, he should

> 'Go round the wood, and round the wood,
> And pick the crooked stick at last.'

Morally he did pick the crooked stick.

He had offered a title for Holy Orders, and the candidate he selected in due course offered himself to the Bishop of the diocese for ordination.

Then came the rub.

Stephen Dashwood, the candidate selected, was a University man, who had taken a good degree in the Natural Science Tripos; he had taken a First Class; he had done exceptionally well. It is not an easy Tripos to take a First in: many of the best men, the very best men, the shining lights of the age, have only taken a Second Class; the subjects it embraces are so many, and so wide, practically it has no limits; and Stephen Dashwood, who had applied to Tom Banister for a title for Orders, for a curacy on a paltry stipend of one hundred pounds a year, had taken a First Class!

Why did he choose the Church? Why didn't he stick to his science?

There was yet time for him to go back; a stumbling-block had already been thrown across the threshold he was so anxious to cross.

When he applied to his tutor for the customary documents to send to the Bishop's chaplain, college testimonials were refused to him.

He wrote to Tom Banister apprising him of the fact. The letter, written under such humiliating circumstances, touched him deeply.

Tom remembered his own youth, and he had a very tender heart. He wrote at once to Dashwood's tutor for an explanation of the reasons for the usual testimonials being withheld.

He received a reply by return of post—a courteous cut-and-dried reply—stating that Mr. Dashwood had not kept the requisite number of college chapels, had not presented himself at the Lord's Table at the prescribed periods, had been 'sent down' two terms, and had not during his residence at the University given unmixed satisfaction to the college authorities, and, under these circumstances, they felt themselves fully justified in taking the extreme measure of placing a bar across the threshold of his professional career.

In most cases it would have been an insuperable bar, and a useful and honourable profession would have been closed against him.

Banister thought he knew his man ; and he knew something of the even-handed justice of alma mater. He remembered his own old college days. He sent the tutor's letter off by the next post to his would-be curate, and requested an explanation of the charges brought against him.

He got the explanation by return.

Such a thorough, open, candid, outspoken confession, made by one erring human creature to another, he had never read. It shamed him to his very soul that such a confession should have been made to him.

And, after all, what were the youthful follies that Dashwood confessed ?

Banister had been guilty of them all in his time ; and he could name men of his own year whose souls were dyed with sins—real sins, ten thousand times deeper than these youthful excesses — who had contrived to keep their chapels, and had been dismissed by alma mater with a benediction accrediting them with eminent Christian graces, and witnessing that they had led virtuous lives, and had been diligent students in many branches of knowledge.

He could recall dozens of these virtuous youths, who had squandered their money in wicked and foolish excesses, and wasted their terms, taking Poll degrees, and coming out at the tail of the Third Class—and his man had taken a First in a Tripos.

He was deeply moved by Stephen Dashwood's manly, straightforward letter. The confession of weakness and folly was so frank, and there was no justification pleaded. He had not, he stated in his letter to Banister, in those thoughtless college days, any intention whatever of entering the Church as a profession. In fact, there were obstacles in the way. He had, like many other students of science, scruples and doubts—serious doubts. Thank Heaven they were all cleared away now, and he had come to his right mind. While they were still with him he could not conscientiously approach the Lord's Table. The call had not come to him until later, when those stormy undergraduate days were over. It had come to him at his mother's death. He

had promised her, at her dying request, that
he would consecrate all the powers God had
given him to His service. The call had
come to him at this solemn time, clear and
imperative and unmistakable. It had come
to him with such insistence that he had
thrown aside all worldly considerations, and
risen up at once to follow the Master who
had so distinctly called him.

No one could have read that deeply
moving letter and doubted the sincerity of
Stephen Dashwood's conversion.

Banister sent his letter to the Bishop's
chaplain, and the Bishop accepted him without further question. Two days after his
ordination Dashwood came to Thorpe Regis
as the curate of St. Michael's.

CHAPTER II.

THE CURATE OF ST. MICHAEL'S.

Tom Banister's wife never could understand why, with so many applications for the
vacant curacy from men with unexceptional
characters and quite immaculate University
careers, her husband should have gone out
of his way to pick a black sheep.

'I wonder what your new curate will be
like, Tom,' Mrs. Banister said at lunch on
the day when Dashwood was expected;
'will he be *very* wicked-looking, and frighten
the congregation into fits?'

Mrs. Banister had an exaggerated way of
putting things.

' Why should he be at all wicked-looking, darling ?' asked the Rector.

He always called his lovely wife ' darling,' and the name suited her.   It suited her, to use the expressive phrase of colloquial slang, down to the ground.

She was as lovely now as the day he married her, seven years ago, when she was the acknowledged belle of the county, and— which was saying a great deal—she was as sweet as she was lovely.   He could not have found a better name for her than ' darling.'

' Oh, because he's got such a bad character.   He couldn't be such a black sheep without showing it.   I expect he'll have a sinister expression—I wonder what a sinister expression is like ?—and I shouldn't be surprised if he had horns somewhere.'

' Darling, you'll frighten the children if you say such things.   Just look at Poppy's face !'

Poppy's face was worth looking at. It was the exact counterpart of her beautiful mother's, only it was smaller and rounder and pinker. Not very much pinker. There was the flush of the wild-rose on Mrs. Tom Banister's cheeks that beat all the rouge in the world, but Poppy's eyes were bluer and rounder, and the hair was a paler flaxen. It was such pretty fluffy flaxen hair, and it framed her dear soft little pink face in an aureole of shining gold.

The blue eyes were opened now to their widest ; they were quite round with wonder.

'It's daddy's black sheep we are talking about, Poppy,' Mrs. Tom explained. 'Haven't you seen their dear black faces and their little horns ?'

'Big horns,' corrected Poppy ; 'great— big—big horns !'

'Black face, black nose, black eyes, black feets ! Ba, ba, black sheep !' added Tommykin, who was a small edition of Poppy, only pinker and rounder and curlier.

The Rector drove over in the dog-cart to the railway-station two miles off, to meet his new curate, and Mrs. Tom and the children accompanied him to the Rectory gate.

'Not now, Poppy; not now, Tommykin!' said the Rector as he drove off, nodding to the children on the path, who were stretching out their little arms to be lifted up on the seat beside him. 'Not now; daddy's going to fetch the black sheep!'

He heard their voices crying after him down the road, 'Bring him back soon, dada! Ba, ba, black sheep!'

It was not difficult to identify the new curate among the little crowd of passengers that came into Thorpe Station by the after-noon train.

Banister saw him the moment the train

stopped, as he stepped out of a third-class carriage. The new curate ought to have looked round for his Rector, who he knew very well was coming to meet him ; but he did nothing of the kind. He stood at the door of the third-class carriage and lifted out an innumerable quantity of bundles and baskets, and finally he helped out a young woman encumbered with a baby and a bird-cage.

He held the baby while she got the bird-cage out of the carriage, and collected together her miscellaneous luggage.

He was still holding the baby when Banister came up to him on the platform, and he had to change the baby from the right arm to the left before he could shake hands with him.

He was a tall, slender young man, rather stooping in his gait, with a plain, sallow face and thin, clear-cut, nervous lips ; but he had

the kindest eyes that Tom had ever seen—
eyes that looked straight out at him with a
look he could almost feel.

No; he was not disappointed in his man.

'Now, is there anything more I can do for
you?' the curate said, when the first greeting
was over.

He was not addressing his Rector; he
was speaking to the woman whose baby he
still held.

She was a young thing, and evidently not
used to travelling; and she stood on the
platform in the midst of her numerous
impedimenta, flushed and bewildered, and
making no effort to take her baby from the
curate's arms.

'I expected my husband would be here to
meet me,' she said, looking helplessly around
at the fast-disappearing crowd. 'He said he
would be here, and bring a donkey and cart
for the things.'

' Have you far to go ?' asked the Rector.

He felt he must say something, and put an end to this absurd situation.

' About three miles, sir,' answered the woman, dropping a curtsey, but making no attempt to take the baby. ' My husband's got a situation at Meadowsweet Farm, Mr. Giles's place, and he's sent for me an' the things. He ought by rights to be here to meet me.'

Meadowsweet Farm was in Tom Banister's parish, and he remembered that he had heard that Giles had recently taken on a fresh labourer, and that a cottage about a mile the other side of Thorpe Regis was being done up for the man's wife and family, who were coming to him from another part of the country.

This, then, was the man's wife, and the new curate was holding the family.

He was not holding all the family ; there

was a bird in a big wicker cage, tied up in a coloured pocket-handkerchief, and there was a cat in a basket, trying very hard to get out, and there was no husband and no donkey-cart to meet them.

The woman was very near crying. She had no money, and she had nowhere to go ; and she stood pale and bewildered among her humble *penates*, looking helplessly around the deserted platform.

The station was quite deserted now, with the exception of the little group among the woman's shabby nondescript luggage. The porters were grinning behind their trucks, and the station-master was watching them from the door of his private office, and the new curate was holding the baby.

It was a most undignified situation.

'I will drive over to Mr. Giles's as I go back,' said Banister, 'and ask him to send a cart to fetch you.'

'Does it lie in our way?' said Dashwood
eagerly. 'How very fortunate! It'll be
quite as easy to take the woman up, and
drop her at her own door. She's had a long
journey already, and with all these things!'

He looked down at the bundles and
baskets on the platform as he spoke; the
cat had already got her head out of one of
them, and was struggling wildly to get free.

'I don't think there's room for all this
luggage,' Banister pleaded weakly, catching
at the first excuse that presented itself.

'Oh yes, there is,' said the curate cheerfully—'plenty of room. My luggage 'll go
anywhere. I've nothing but a portmanteau
and a dog.'

Tom hadn't noticed the dog until Dashwood mentioned it, and, as he spoke, a sleek
shiny little black-and-white fox-terrier crept
out from between his legs and began barking
at the cat.

Without any further permission on the
Rector's part, the woman's miscellaneous
bundles were thrown into the dog-cart, and
the woman herself was helped up into the
front seat beside him. She couldn't ride on
the back seat, she said, with a baby in her
arms ; she was quite sure she should fall
out.

The curate, who had superintended the
transfer of the luggage, brought up the rear
with the baby, and, having resigned his
charge at last, jumped up behind and drove
into Thorpe Regis with a birdcage between
his legs, and his entire attention for the re-
mainder of the journey concentrated upon
keeping the recalcitrant cat within the
basket, from which it was wildly struggling
to get free.

It was not at all a dignified introduction to
his new parish. Everybody they met on the
way no doubt thought that it was *his* wife,

and *his* baby, and *his* birdcage in that red
pocket-handkerchief, and that he was dreadfully ill-using the cat.

After this absurd exhibition, Banister was
prepared for any amount of quixotism in his
new curate. Perhaps because he was prepared for it, he was a little disappointed
because Dashwood behaved very much like
other men. If he went about the parish
carrying babies, and helping lame dogs over
stiles, he did it when no one was by. He
created no open scandal.

The Rector's pretty wife, who happened
to be waiting at the Rectory gate when the
cavalcade drove by, was never tired of telling
the tale of her husband's discomfiture. She
used to tell it at every tea-table in Thorpe,
and draw a long face and pucker her smooth
forehead to show how Tom looked when the
baby squealed, and the terrier, perched on the
top of the bundles, yelped, and the cat, with

her head out of the basket, used very un-parliamentary language.

Oh the fun Mrs. Tom made of that un-lucky journey, and how she teased poor Tom about it! She took the new curate up at once on the strength of it. She was rather fond of black sheep, if the truth must be told. She was so sick of proper people; they were the bane of her life. There were at least a dozen old women in Thorpe Regis that she positively hated. They were always preaching at her—they never ventured to preach to her—and she had to sit and eat their bread-and-butter, and drink their un-sweetened tea, and smile in their glum faces like an angel.

A rector's wife cannot pick her friends like the wives of members of any other learned profession—a doctor's or a lawyer's, for instance. They may have cliques, but a rector's wife mustn't be cliquey. She must be civil to everybody, and well for her if she can meet the impertinences of ill-natured, odious people with the smile of an angel.

Mrs. Banister introduced her husband's new curate to the select society of Thorpe at a tennis-party.

If she had been a right-minded clergyman's wife, she ought to have got up a parish tea, or some other solemn function; and there ought to have been some hymns sung, and the new deacon ought to have gone round, properly dressed in sober clerical habiliments, and shaken hands. But Mrs. Tom was not right-minded; she was young and frivolous, and human—very human— and she preferred tennis to prayer meetings.

She asked quite a large party to meet the new curate. She was helping Tom to mark out the two tennis-courts on the lawn, and put up the nets, and roll the grass, all the morning. Most people would have let the

gardener do it, but Laura Banister was fond
of doing that sort of thing herself. She was
never happier than when she had a racket in
her hand, and was skipping in a most undignified way about a tennis-court.

She was jumping about like any girl of
sixteen in one of the courts she had marked
out, with the curate for her *vis-à-vis*, when
her visitors began to arrive.

One can't jump about in a long-tailed
coat, with a clerical waistcoat buttoned up to
the throat beneath it. The dignity of the
Church would be at stake.

Hence Stephen Dashwood's first introduction to Thorpe Regis and his new parishioners was in flannels. It was a dreadfully
hot July day, and hopping about in the sun
was hot work.

The warm, perspiring man that Mrs.
Banister introduced to her friends didn't look
the least like a curate.

His throat was open—a very fine, manly throat it was, and as fair as a woman's ; and his dark, crisp, curling hair was thrown back off his forehead ; his eyes—they were very dark gray-blue eyes, and they were rather fine eyes—were shining with excitement, and his face was pink with heat, and decidedly damp with the exercise.

Dashwood had to submit to such a lot of introductions : he had to keep leaving off a game to be introduced to somebody. There were only women to be introduced to, so that he couldn't give just a casual nod and go on with his game.

There were very few men for Mrs. Tom to present. Whatever sons or brothers there were belonging to Thorpe Regis society were drafted off to London, or some other big centre, as soon as they were of an age to leave the paternal roof. There was nothing for young men to do in Thorpe,

except play lawn-tennis, and smoke, and
' hang around.'

It was not a wealthy community, and the
male population was distributed over the face
of the globe in the capacity of bank clerks,
law and medical students, cadets, ensigns,
and civil servants, and a small percentage
were roughing it in the Bush.

It was a great pity the girls couldn't have
been drafted off in a similar way. There
was really nothing for them to do from
morning till night but play croquet or tennis,
or make calls and talk scandal, or fall ill and
have the medical Adonis of the neighbourhood called in to prescribe for them.

Stephen Dashwood was introduced to
dozens of girls that afternoon. They had all
put on new summer dresses to meet him. The
Rectory lawn had never been so besprinkled
with gay colours and dainty toilettes before.
It really looked like a bed of poppies.

It was a blue July day, and there wasn't a cloud in the sky, and the midsummer sun was blazing down upon the lawn, and upon the girls in their fresh summer frocks.

Nobody would have expected them to have come dressed in a sack on such a day as this, but it was remarkable the singular unanimity with which they had all put on their most becoming gowns to meet the new curate.

He had his work cut out to satisfy them all. He didn't sit down once that afternoon, but played religiously in every set until the blessed respite for tea.

No wonder he was pink and perspiring. He plumped down on a low grassy bank in the delicious shade, and the girl he had been playing with plumped down beside him, and all the other girls looked on.

She was pink too, or red, rather, and she wore a red gown--at least, a white top and a red skirt—and she had very soft dark eyes and golden-brown hair, and a sweet, reedy voice, and she played tennis beautifully.

'I am so glad you've come, Mr. Dashwood,' she was saying in her confidential, free-and-easy way, as if she had known him for years; 'now we shall have someone to play with. It's been awfully slow having nothing but girls. I'm quite sick of girls!'

'Really!' said the curate. He didn't know what else to say.

'Yes; we are all girls or old women in Thorpe. We have no one on earth to say a word to us.'

'Haven't you any brothers?'

'No, I haven't got a brother; but that doesn't matter. I prefer other people's brothers.'

The sentiment was not a new one, but Stephen had seldom heard it so freely expressed.

'And have not the other people got any brothers?' he asked with a laugh.

'Oh yes ; but none of any good. All that are worth anything go away. I hope we shall have plenty of tennis-parties and con-certs and dances now you have come. I hope you dance?'

The curate opened his eyes and looked steadily at his interlocutor.

'Yes,' he said slowly, 'I dance, certainly ; at least, I have been used to dancing, but I have not tried it yet in a clerical evening coat.'

Then, to his great relief, Mrs. Banister came and took him away.

'How could you talk to that horrid girl?' she said, as she walked back to the house with him across the grass. 'We could hear her shouting the other side of the lawn.'

'I'm afraid she talked to me,' he said weakly. 'If you hadn't come in time and carried me away, I believe she would have made me stand up and dance.'

There were at least twenty people that Mrs. Tom was anxious to introduce her husband's new curate to, and this minx—she called her a minx—of a Dolly Grove was taking up all his attention, and making a spectacle of herself lolling on the grass beside him in her scarlet gown.

She didn't carry him away a minute too soon. Every lady on the lawn, which really meant everybody in Thorpe, vowed he was flirting in the most barefaced way with that forward Miss Grove. He made a dozen enemies that unlucky afternoon, and set all the tongues in Thorpe wagging.

It was a very bad beginning for a new curate.

CHAPTER III.

THE tennis-party was a mistake, Mrs. Tom acknowledged with a sigh.

That horrid girl had spoilt it.

Everybody had gone away with the impression that Stephen Dashwood had been flirting with Dolly Grove. She was a bold, designing, forward minx, so Mrs. Tom said to herself; she laid herself out to entrap every man that came to Thorpe.

She had done her best to entrap the last curate, and now that he had gone away, she was making an audacious attempt upon his successor.

It was very lucky that she had gone up when she did and carried him away. He was evidently a weak-minded young man, and would fall an easy prey to any woman. Having once set her heart upon anything, Mrs. Tom moved heaven and earth to accomplish it. She never did anything by halves.

She had made up her mind that the new curate should be a success ; she had taken to him from that first moment when she saw him driving by the Rectory gate, with a birdcage between his legs, and expostulating with the cat.

Nothing could have made her more angry than this mistaken impression that the scandal - loving people of Thorpe carried away with them.

She thanked Heaven that she hadn't asked the Bulstrode Court set. She only asked the Bulstrode people to very exclusive functions—a quiet afternoon tea, or a small, very small, dinner-party. There were not many people in Thorpe Lady Camilla Bulstrode cared to meet.

Lady Camilla was the wife of the Member for the Northern Division of the county, and lived in the great house two miles away from Thorpe Regis. Sir Probyn Bulstrode was the Master of the Foxhounds ; he didn't care for many things in life except hunting and shooting and Parliamentary debates. Besides Bulstrode Court and a shooting-box in the Highlands, he had a fine house in town.

Between the long Parliamentary session and the shooting in the Highlands, Sir Probyn did not spend very much of the year at Thorpe.

When the family were at Bulstrode the house was generally filled with guests, and then a mild round of dissipation sustained the drooping relations of the Court with the county.

The family were at the Court now. Lady Camilla had come down a week or two before the end of the season, fagged out, and had left Sir Probyn in town, working like a horse at his Parliamentary committees.

Her ladyship was not so young now as she once was, and she couldn't go through the treadmill of a London season without getting a little fagged towards its close.

She was fagged earlier than usual this year, and she had come down a fortnight sooner. Mrs. Tom was very anxious that Dashwood should create a favourable impression on Lady Camilla. So much depended on her verdict. The little world of Thorpe Regis worshipped her, and accepted her judgment as gospel. Whoever she took up they admired with slavish admiration ; whoever she put down they immediately sat upon.

She took up very funny people sometimes. Mrs. Tom did not tell Stephen the good fortune that awaited him when she asked him to come in to afternoon tea a few days after that ill-starred tennis-party. She did not tell him who he was going to meet.

He might have been too much elated. He forgot all about the afternoon tea until long past five o'clock, and then he was in two minds about going. He had been visiting all the afternoon, and was hot and tired and dusty.

It was a dreadfully hot day, and the dust was intolerable. He was not really fit to go into anybody's room.

Stephen Dashwood shook off as much of the dust he had brought in with him from the dusty country roads as he could in the hall of the Rectory, and then he followed the prim parlourmaid into the drawing-room. It was so dark and cool here in the carefully shaded room that, coming in from the white glare of the sun, he could not for a few moments distinguish that there was anybody in the room besides the Rector's wife at the tea-table.

She rose up when he came in, and introduced him to her visitors.

He couldn't see them very well ; his eyes had not got accustomed to the light—to the shade, rather—but he became aware that he was in the august presence of the great people from the Court.

He was rather thankful for the dusky twilight of the room ; they couldn't see how dusty he was.

'I am sorry to be so late,' he said, addressing Mrs. Tom. 'I have been visiting all the afternoon, and I forgot all about the time.'

' I am glad you find the people so absorbing,' Mrs. Tom said, with a laugh. ' How you must have enjoyed them to have forgotten your tea!'

Stephen took the rebuke meekly.

' I have been breaking new ground. I have found out a place called Littlecourt, with quite a population of its own.'

' Littlecourt?' said Lady Camilla. ' Oh, that's our place. All the workpeople live at Littlecourt. I believe it's a horrible place!'

Stephen looked at the speaker, a large, well-preserved woman, who not only had been a beauty, but was a beauty still. A great thing to say for a woman who has a grown-up daughter—a daughter as tall as herself, and promising to be as handsome.

Stephen looked her ladyship in the face; he could not help even then remarking how fair it was, and how well preserved; and then he said very distinctly:

'Yes, you are quite right ; it is horrible !'

Mrs. Tom looked up from the teacups ; she thought Dashwood had put his foot in it, but Lady Camilla laughed outright.

'Horrible isn't the word,' she said ; 'it's frightful ! All the scum of the county seem to collect there. Sir Probyn asks such a ridiculous rent for the cottages that the place is full of people who ought to be in the union.'

'Not your own people ?'

'Oh dear no ! A lot of our workpeople live there, but the rest of the cottages are let to strangers. Sir Probyn has given them all notice to quit, but it is of no use ; they won't go, and he can't turn them into the road. The only thing he can do is to pull the houses down about their ears.'

'The very best thing he can do, if he will build up some others first.'

And then Dashwood thought he had said quite enough about the Littlecourt property,

and he got up to take Miss Bulstrode's cup
and saucer.

She was younger than her mother, and
that was all that could be said about her.
In the dusky light of that shaded room she
did not look a year younger.

She had a very low voice, which we know
is an excellent thing in woman ; and Lady
Camilla had a loud voice, and that was very
nearly all the difference.

Having relieved her of her cup and saucer,
Dashwood sat down beside her, and presently he found her asking him questions in
her low, soft, patrician voice about the place
and the people. He answered her in his
outspoken way, as he had answered Lady
Camilla ; he did not see the necessity for
any reserve.

'I think the life of the country is intolerable,' he was saying ; 'it is worse than it is
in towns. There there are always some

distractions ; but here there is nothing, nothing but the tap-room of a village inn. Oh, how can we expect people to be better than the animals, living as they do ?'

'What would you do to improve them ?' Miss Bulstrode asked.

' Do ? I would teach them how to live, to begin with.'

' You would set up more schools ?'

' No ; I wouldn't set up more schools : they have quite enough schools ; but I would teach them something beyond the three R's. I would go even beyond the sixth standard.'

' I think they have got beyond that already. I heard mamma say that the piano was being taught in Board schools in some places, and that the housemaids were going to learn drawing.'

' They might learn a great many worse things ; but that is scarcely what I mean. They will never attain any proficiency in

music or drawing—never enough to get any
real pleasure or benefit out of it. I would
teach them to read and to think—to exercise
their brains as well as their muscles. I
would give them recreation in the true and
literal sense of the word.'

'What *are* you talking about?' said her
ladyship across the room. She was not
accustomed to being ignored.

'We were talking about amusing the
people, mamma,' said Miss Bulstrode, sup-
pressing a yawn. 'Mr. Dashwood doesn't
think music and drawing will satisfy them.
He thinks they ought to be amused.'

'Miss Bulstrode is right,' said Stephen,
addressing Lady Camilla, who was looking
at him through her long eyeglass as if he
were some strange animal. 'I think the
people want to be amused. They work very
hard all day, and at night they have nothing
to fall back upon but the public-house.'

' I am sure they are quite satisfied with
the public-house. There is nothing they
like so well as getting tipsy.'

' Exactly ; they drink to drive away dul-
ness. They have nothing else to do. They
have nothing in the world to think about but
what they have done to-day, and what they
are going to do to-morrow. They have no
tastes, and they have no occupations. They
have no means of recreating the exhausted
mind at the end of the day but such means
as are open to them in the village tap-
room.'

' I don't see how you are to amuse them
if they have no tastes,' said Lady Camilla,
with some show of interest.

Really this young man was quite amusing.
Mrs. Tom had been telling her about that
absurd spectacle of the baby and the bird-
cage, and Lady Camilla never lost a chance
of amusing herself at anybody's expense.

She was not at all particular. The new curate was as good as a show.

' We should have to create the taste,' said Stephen quite coolly, as if he took her remark *au sérieux*. ' I don't think we should have had any tastes ourselves, except, indeed, the baser sort, if they hadn't been cultivated. The refinement that we pride ourselves upon, I take it, has nothing to do with our tastes, but is due to the nature and variety of our occupations. If working people had something else to do of nights, they would not fall back upon the tap-room.'

' What would you give them to do ?'

' I would teach the men athletics, to begin with ; I would give them simple lectures on natural science, literature, poetry, travels. I would teach the girls dancing, singing, tennis, croquet. I would teach them such things as would bring out and develop all the higher faculties of body and mind.'

Stephen was very much in earnest; his eyes were shining and his lips were eloquent. Lady Camilla was not only amused, she was quite interested in him.

'You must come over to Bulstrode, Mr. Dashwood, and tell me more of your wonderful projects,' she said good-naturedly; and then she got up and said good-bye to Mrs. Tom.

Stephen helped her into her little low pony-carriage, and she gave him her hand at parting; and Miss Bulstrode nodded to him, and told him to be sure to come soon.

Stephen thought he had done a great thing in enlisting the interest of the great people of Thorpe in his pet projects; but Mrs. Tom shook her head.

'I'm afraid you've put your foot in it,' she said darkly. 'Lady Camilla hasn't a scrap of interest in the people. She comes of one of the oldest Tory families in the kingdom,

who believe it would create nothing short of
a revolution in the country if you were to
teach working men and women to dance.
I'm sorry you mentioned those cottages, too,
at Littlecourt. Sir Probyn never troubles
about the property ; he leaves everything to
his steward.'

Mrs. Tom for once in her life reckoned
without her host.

Lady Camilla took to the dancing project
immensely. Tory as she was, she was always
seeking after something new, and here was
something quite, quite new—an untried ex-
periment.

She invited Stephen to Bulstrode before
the week was over, and talked over his
Utopian schemes for the higher education
of the people with him.

Lady Camilla quite caught his enthusiasm.
She took up 'fads' very quickly, and she
dropped them with equal readiness ; she

would begin at once, and make the lives of the poor people of Thorpe lovely and gracious and refined. She hardly knew where to begin, and she certainly did not know where to stop.

Stephen would have suggested building some new cottages at Littlecourt, and pulling down the old ones ; but that was Sir Probyn's work, and a reference to the subject might have damped her ardour. He let her go her own way. Within a month of the day that Stephen had broached the subject to her, the foundations had been laid for a big parish hall, which was to be wholly given up to social amusements for the people. Here concerts were to be held, and lectures given, and singing taught, and dancing— *real* dancing. A lady was to be brought down from London on purpose to teach dancing, and a bandmaster from the neighbouring city was to teach music—drum, fife, sackbut, and all manner of music. There was to be a regular orchestra.

Lady Camilla's philanthropy did not stop with the dancing. She shocked the sensibilities of the small gentry of Thorpe Regis, who drew a line of demarcation between the amusements of the upper and the lower classes, by laying out a ground for tennis, and providing nets and rackets for the use of the people.

Oh, it was going too far!

Croquet would have been all very well, and bowls, and skittles for the men, and cricket—they had these, besides—but tennis! Lady Camilla was certainly going too far.

Everybody blamed Stephen for leading her ladyship on. There were so many other things wanted in the parish more than a tennis-ground and a dancing-booth. A hospital was sadly needed, and new schools, and a mission-room at the farther end of the

parish ; and the winter would be coming on
soon, and there would be blankets and fuel
and beef for the poor wanted. Oh, it was
a great waste of money !

Stephen threw himself into all these
schemes of Lady Camilla's with all his heart,
while his Rector looked on with a certain
amount of disfavour and suspicion.

He would have interfered about the dancing
—he drew a line at the dancing, as the ladies
had drawn a line at the tennis—but for Mrs.
Tom. Lady Camilla had won her over, and
Mrs. Tom, as everybody knew, ruled the
parish by proxy ; so the great recreation
scheme was allowed to go on unchecked.

No one could say that the new curate
neglected his work, his visiting, and his
clubs and his services, for these Arcadian
schemes. He did his duty as thoroughly as
his predecessor, the model curate, and he
found leisure to carry out Lady Camilla's

programme ; but everybody said that he had turned the parish upside down.

The visiting ladies who went round with a little bag for the clothing club pennies, and distributed tracts on the immorality of dancing and such frivolous amusements, complained that he had spoiled the *morale* of the people.

Some ladies went so far as to say that the Bishop had made a great mistake in admitting a young man with such worldly views into the Church, and that old story of the black sheep, which Mrs. Tom had dropped accidentally at a tea-party, was revived with additions.

There was no doubt that Mr. Banister, among all his candidates, had chosen the black sheep.

CHAPTER IV.

THORPE REGIS was a delightful little country town, just large enough to mind its own business, but not too large for gossip and slander.

There was a broad, sunny High Street, with a bank, and a post-office, and a town-hall, and a fair sprinkling of shops. There were still a few old-fashioned red-bricked houses abutting on the street as they used to do in the old days. These were generally distinguished by immaculate white doorsteps and shining brass knockers ; and one or two —the doctor's and the lawyer's—had a row of green posts in front, with chains festooned between, to keep off cattle, perhaps, or to add dignity to the tenements they protected.

There was a delightful shady street that led out of the High Street, up a rather steep hill to the church, and here the *élite* of Thorpe Regis lived. People like to congregate round a church. The people who lived in this delightful street could see the gray tower every time they looked out of their windows, and the cawing of the rooks in the old elms in the churchyard woke them up betimes every morning, and the church-bell — it was a very sweet-toned old bell — called them to matins every day ; to busy people that bell seemed to be never still. It was always chiming the hours and the half-hours and the quarters, and the ringers were always ready for any excuse to ring a peal.

The houses in Church Street stood well
away from the road—modest little houses,
buried in greenery, and covered with
creepers, and embosomed in flowers. The
Rectory was not far off from the church ;
a gate from the Rectory garden led into the
churchyard, but it was a long garden, and
there were delightful orchard lawns spreading
between it and the church.

There were a number of other unimportant
narrow winding streets, all uphill and down-
hill, and leading to nowhere particular ; and
in the lower part of the town, near the river,
was a woollen factory that employed several
hundred hands. It was a decayed old town,
and in the old part, beyond the church and
the Rectory, were still standing some dilapidated old-fashioned houses, that had once
been the residences of the wealthy in-
habitants of Thorpe. Fashion had removed
now to Church Street, and Ring's End, as

this part of the parish was called, probably from its proximity to the old bull-ring, was deserted.

Some of the old houses were divided off and let to poorer tenants, and others were empty and falling to decay. One of these houses, to the surprise of everybody, had been let, about a twelvemonth before Stephen came to Thorpe, to a lady of title— a Russian Baroness, it was reported.

Very few people would have cared to take the gloomy old house. It stood a long way back from the road, and was approached by a path through a dense shrubbery, which hadn't been trimmed or attended to for years. This cavernous-like entrance opened out upon a lawn surrounded by gloomy old trees ; the house itself was covered with ivy and creepers, and was about as damp and depressing a place as could be well found, and it was in dreadfully bad repair.

The first thing the Baroness von Eberlein
did was to alter the name of the house from
Rus in Urbe to the Hermitage, and then she
set about furnishing it.

Nobody seemed to know where she came
from.   She came quite suddenly ; she might
have dropped down from the skies.   She
brought an old servant with her, and a
young girl—a companion—who was said to
be a cousin, and—and half a dozen cats.

There was no doubt about the cats.   No
other inhabitant of the Hermitage could be
seen over that jealous wall that shut it out
so completely from the road, but the cats
were seen on the wall taking an airing by
day, and heard taking part in a concert by
night.   Some people averred that they had
counted twelve cats on the wall at one time,
and others were prepared to state that they
had heard—distinctly heard—and identified
twelve separate voices in these midnight

performances of the Ring's End Harmonic
Society.

The Baroness von Eberlein, though she
retained her title, had dropped the trappings
and surroundings of rank. She had brought
only one female servant with her—an old
woman, lean and brown, and wrinkled like
an autumn pear, who could not speak a
word of English, and she had not engaged
any Thorpe servants. She had brought
with her, besides, an old piebald pony, and
had hired a low pony carriage, and engaged
a small boy from the country to look after it.
She had put the boy into livery, with a big
coronet on every one of his shining gilt
buttons. The page-boy and the old woman
comprised the entire establishment of the
Hermitage.

The Baroness was as remarkable as her
surroundings.

She was a widow—a fair white plump

widow—decidedly plump, but not fat. A
woman made on a grand scale, not *petite*
by any means, and not a giantess—a woman
of middle height, with a fine figure, and
handsome arms that her perfectly fitting
dress showed to perfection, and a handsome
bust that it also displayed in the same liberal
spirit.

She might be any age from twenty to
forty ; her face was an unusual one, and
not without attraction—a dead white, waxen
complexion, soft and white and velvety,
with pale-brown eyebrows strongly marked,
and pale-brown chestnut hair, and full red
lips ; a strong mouth — strong and wide,
almost too wide for perfect beauty—and a
nose of no distinct type, and decidedly
retroussé.

It was her distinctive feature, and it
marred what might have been a beautiful
face. The colouring of the face was remark-

able—chestnut hair and amber eyes, and a waxen, creamy complexion.

Her eyes were soft and sleepy, and she did not often open them wide enough for their unusual colour to be seen; but when she did open them they were yellow—tawny golden yellow—like a tiger's.

No one was quite sure of her nationality. She was not English, everyone agreed; she might be German, or French, or Italian, or Russian—most likely Russian. As no one in Thorpe had ever seen a subject of the Czar's, and the stranger's unusual appearance did not correspond to any familiar type they were acquainted with, with general consent she was voted Russian.

And if Russian, probably a Nihilist seeking refuge in England, perhaps plotting secretly in the seclusion of the Hermitage.

This suggestion explained everything:

the seclusion, the mysterious dropping down from the clouds, the absence of antecedents, the smallness of the establishment. It explained everything but the cats.

The Baroness gave no references; she paid the landlord of the Hermitage half a year's rent in advance, and she paid the tradespeople liberally. There was no lack of money; the establishment was not restricted to one old servant and a page-boy for lack of means.

People called on the Baroness when she first came to the Hermitage, the Rector's wife among them, and for a time she created quite a flutter in the little exclusive society of Thorpe Regis.

But the acquaintance never went any farther, never ripened into friendships. People were afraid of her. Perhaps they discovered something lacking—they were not accustomed to the society of Russian Baronesses and Nihilists—and she never talked about her husband.

Women are so much quicker to find out things about each other than men—quicker to suspect, and quicker to put things together and form conclusions.

They would have liked to have known more about her, but the Baroness had a way of parrying inquiries that baffled all their ingenuity.

She refused to gratify their curiosity; she paid her way, and she outraged no social laws; she had a right to live as she liked, and keep a dozen cats and no servants to speak of, and have an entrance to her house as dark as Avernus.

She dressed beautifully, both she and her companion, her cousin Bébée, as she called the girl she had brought with her. The Baroness always dressed in dark rich colours that set off the creamy, waxen whiteness of her marvellous complexion, and Bébée wore light delicate tints and flimsy materials, made in an old - world, childish fashion that Kate Greenaway has made popular—a fashion that suited well her ridiculous name and her unformed, gawkish figure.

She was a namby-pamby creature, child or woman ; pale and puny, with pink circles round her eyes, which were very light in colour—a light gray-green, decidedly green in some lights—and she had pale-pink lips, and drab hair, and drab eyelashes, and deplorable teeth. She bore a distinct re-semblance to a white mouse.

She was a washed - out edition of the Baroness, a pale, spiritless creature, with a shy, frightened, timid manner. It was rumoured that the Baroness bullied her dreadfully in secret. Screams had been heard proceeding from the back regions of that mysterious house after dark—screams, and hysterical sobbing and wild appeals for help.

The Baroness Eberlein had explained, when questioned about these sounds, that Bébée was hysterical, and that she was a martyr to neuralgia.

The girls of Thorpe Regis, who were not ill-natured, would have taken up poor Bébée, but she was such a shy, frightened creature ; she would not stir an inch without her kinswoman.

' I am sure she treats that poor little thing shamefully, and beats her black and blue,' a girl who had caught Bébée weeping surreptitiously in church said at an afternoon tea ; and forthwith everybody in Thorpe agreed that the Baroness was a female Bluebeard, and that she had a secret chamber in the Hermitage full of murdered

Bébées, or as much of them as the cats had not consumed.

The Baroness and her companion were always in their seat at church—the front seat ; they were the most regular of the small select congregation who attended the daily services.

The Rector ought to have made more of them, for the Baroness's purse was always open to every charitable call that was made upon it. She subscribed liberally to all the local charities, and she put half-crowns in the plate in church when other people put in sixpences.

Still, in spite of the half-crowns and the regular attendance at the daily services, the Rector's wife cooled after a short acquaintance with Baroness Eberlein.

Then other people began to cool, but not all at once. They found out, or thought they found out, certain indications lacking of—well, of gentle breeding.

And they couldn't hear anything of the Baroness's late husband.

It was while her friends were falling away from her, and stories—rather ugly stories— were being whispered about her, that Stephen Dashwood came as curate to Thorpe Regis.

It was quite by accident Stephen called at the Hermitage in the quite early days of his parochial visits.

He had no list given him by his Rector of the people he ought to visit ; the parish was mapped out into districts, and a district was apportioned to each day. When Ring's End came in turn to be visited, Stephen called upon the Baroness. He had called upon her poorer neighbours on either side, and not recognising any distinction in one decayed-looking old tenement from another, he had penetrated into the very secret recesses of the Hermitage.

He had not gone up to the front-door, as he ought to have done; he had turned to the left instead of turning to the right when he had passed through the gloomy cavern that the people of Thorpe termed Avernus, and he had found his way to the back-door.

He had stumbled over half a dozen cats by the way, and he had penetrated into the kitchen of the Hermitage before he found out his mistake.

It was a large, gloomy kitchen, and it was not remarkably clean, and an old crone, brown and wrinkled, and bent double with age, was preparing some kind of savoury soup over the fire.

Stephen was in the kitchen before she noticed him; she had been so engrossed bending over the pot on the fire that she had not heard him knock at the door.

At the sound of his voice she turned

round and saw him standing in the middle
of the kitchen. It is no unusual thing for
a clergyman to enter a cottage and make
himself at home without very much cere-
mony, and Stephen couldn't understand the
panic that seized the poor old creature when
she saw him standing there.

Her jaw fell, and she raised her hands
with a terror-stricken gesture, and Stephen
saw that she was trembling all over. He
hastened to reassure her, and explained the
nature of his visit; and took out his little
book—he always carried a little black book
with him in these visits — and began to
deliver his message.

He delivered it to unwilling ears. The
old woman was mumbling something he
could not understand, in a barbarous language
he had never heard before, and she was ges-
ticulating wildly in the direction of the door.

He could not mistake her meaning. She

wanted neither him nor his message ; she only wanted him to go.

He wasn't at all sure he hadn't come across a lunatic. He looked helplessly round the kitchen, vaguely wondering whether it were safe for such a person to be at large ; and while he was looking round, an inner door opened and a girl came running in. A pale, frightened girl, crying bitterly, and followed by an enormous fierce-looking black cat.

' Oh, Annette !' cried the girl, ' she has set that brute at me again, and it has bitten my arm——'

She stopped suddenly when she saw Stephen, and she involuntarily made a movement to cover up her arm, which was bleeding profusely, with her hand.

Stephen recognised her in a moment as the girl he had seen in church in the quaint Kate Greenaway gowns.

He came forward at once, and offered his help, and insisted on examining the wounded limb. It was only a little superficial wound, but it was bleeding freely ; and while he was still examining it, the Baroness came in.

She had heard a strange voice in the kitchen, and she came *frou-frouing* with her rich trailing skirts along the passage to see to whom it belonged.

She took in the situation in a moment, and came forward in her delightful frank foreign way and held out her hand to the curate.

'Ah!' she said, smiling, 'you have come in the wrong way. Why, what is the matter with Bébée? Oh, you silly Bébée ; you have been teasing the cats again ! I am always scolding her, Mr. Dashwood '— she knew his name quite well—'for teasing the cats. She is such a child, she can't leave them alone ; and when they scratch her, she begins to cry.'

'I am afraid it is more than a scratch,' said Stephen gravely; 'I think the brute has bitten her.'

'No, no,' said the girl eagerly; 'it is only a scratch. It is not really anything; it was my own fault. I was teasing the cat—and—and it flew at me—and I was frightened.'

'No,' said the Baroness, in her soft, purring voice; 'no, fortunately, it is only a scratch. Poor little Bébée!'

She took out of her pocket a little dainty flimsy handkerchief edged with old Flemish lace, and wound it tenderly round the girl's arm.

'My poor little Bébée!' she said, in her soft, caressing voice; 'did the naughty kitsey-mew scratch her!'

She playfully pinched the girl's pale cheeks and kissed her, and throwing her arm tenderly round her waist, she led her out of the kitchen, and the curate meekly followed them hat in hand.

He forgot all about the old woman and his 'message,' and he slipped the shabby little black book into his pocket.

CHAPTER V.

BARBE BLEUE.

STEPHEN came often to the Hermitage after that day. The acquaintance, begun under such ridiculous circumstances, soon ripened into intimacy.

The Baroness understood him, Stephen found out, and she was interested in all his schemes. She had a delightful caressing way of showing her interest in him that quite won his confidence, and the foolish, impressionable fellow had not known her a month before he had bared his whole heart to her.

She threw her house open to him, and he

went in and out of the Hermitage as if it had been his home.

He hated sitting down to a lonely meal, and there was always a lovely supper, cooked to perfection—rumour said that the Baroness cooked it herself—waiting for him at Ring's End.

There never were such cutlets and curries as the Baroness's, and she always had some delicate French wine to wash them down.

There was every excuse for Stephen finding his way so often from his gloomy lodgings to the Hermitage.

He hated to sit down alone to his solitary mutton-chop—his landlady seldom varied this dainty—and there was never a bottle of French wine in the cellarette of those bare rooms. But it was not altogether for the loaves and fishes that Stephen came over evening after evening to Ring's End. He liked to talk to the Baroness about his

schemes. Lady Camilla had gone away to
Scotland, and there was nobody who took
so much interest in the work as the Baroness.
She entered into everything—the dancing,
and the singing, and the cooking classes;
she was quite ready to help in all.

Stephen never could have got through the
winter without her help; there was nobody
else to stand by him. Everybody said he
was demoralizing the parish. Lady Camilla
did not come back till just before Christmas,
and by that time her enthusiasm had cooled.
The dancing-mistress was not forthcoming,
and the bandmaster did not turn up; and if
the Baroness and Bébée had not helped him
to get up some concerts for the people, the
whole thing would have turned out a failure,
and he would have got well laughed at for
his pains.

He got laughed at as it was.

One can't do very much towards helping

one's fellow - creatures without exciting a
little laughter. People laughed at him for
being mixed up with that foreign woman,
and a great many people who might have
helped him—among them, it was rumoured,
Lady Camilla—held aloof on that account.

The Rector and his wife withdrew entirely
from these recreation schemes when they no
longer had Lady Camilla's countenance ; and
the great room, that was to have been a
dancing-booth and a concert-hall through the
winter, was devoted to lectures and parish
meetings.

Stephen bore the disappointment with an
ill grace ; he could not have borne it at all
if his friends at the Hermitage hadn't comforted him and helped him with their
sympathy. He was one of those ridiculous
young men who wear their hearts upon their
sleeve, and when they get wounded go to the
first woman they meet to bandage them up.

Stephen got a great many wounds during that hard first winter at Thorpe, and he generally went to the Hermitage to get them bound up.

Everything was new and strange to him, and he was so ridiculously thin-skinned and emotional that if anything went wrong in the parish or the church he broke down, and then he wanted a good deal of comforting.

He generally got as much as he wanted —sometimes more. It would have been much better for him, when he was smarting under some fancied slight, if he had gone back to his own rooms and borne his trouble in secret. It would have been healthier and better ; he would have got strength, at any rate, and he would have learnt endurance.

Anything would have been better and more manly than, directly anything went wrong, to go howling up to the Hermitage.

Perhaps it is not fair to condemn him.

There was every excuse for his going up
to the Hermitage so often. The Baroness
understood him. It was more like home to
him — home with its freedom — than any
other place in Thorpe.

He was generally quite tired by the end
of the day ; and, after having had his nerves
strung at tension with the visiting and the
services and the meetings for so many hours,
he was not unwilling to relax a little when
an opportunity came. He was quite ready
to take off his armour when the day's work
was done. He could not always be preaching and praying—at least, he told himself
so, when his conscience took him to task,
as it sometimes did, after these little
suppers. A man must take his armour off
sometimes.

Stephen generally took off his armour—
his spiritual armour—when he got the other
side of Avernus. It would have been quite

out of place in the Baroness's little drawing-room.

A delightful cosy, cushiony little room, with soft carpets and couches and low lounging-chairs—a room where everything seemed to invite repose. It was always exactly the right temperature—not a cold, bare, draughty room like an ice-house—and it was always carefully shaded ; and the air, if not exactly heavy, was odorous with some subtle kind of Eastern perfume, and there was always an enormous black cat drowsing on the hearthrug.

Oh no ! it was not at all the place to wear one's armour in.

After these little suppers there was music ; sometimes the Baroness would sing to him— little sparkling French and German songs— but she preferred to sit in one of the low chairs beside Stephen, and talk to him about his work while Bébée played or sang.

She had a very great interest in his work. She used to make him tell her what he had been doing all day, and whom he had seen ; she might have been his Rector for the account she made him render. While they talked Bébée played a low, soft accompaniment on the piano ; she played beautifully, and she never tired. She played sometimes the whole evening without a pause, and while she played they talked.

She paused sometimes for a moment's rest, and the Baroness would say something in German or Russian — something that sounded very soft and sweet to Stephen, who couldn't understand a word of it—and poor Bébée would begin afresh.

' The child is passionately fond of music,' she used to explain to Stephen, 'and she looks forward to these delightful practices. You are sure you don't mind her practising while you are here ?'

And Stephen, of course, would say ' No.'

She had such a delightful way of showing her interest in Stephen ; only women of a certain age can safely show an interest in a man—a very young man—in this delightful way. It is scarcely maternal, but it is the next thing to it, and it affords endless opportunities for all sorts of little tender offices—little playful, caressing attentions that an old woman can lavish upon a man young enough to be her son.

The Baroness used to call herself an old woman—it was her favourite fiction—at these times, as she sat petting Stephen in the soft, shaded light of the dusky room.

She found out everything about him as she sat there night after night, questioning him in her wheedling way. It was decidedly a wheedling way ; there was no other name for it.

She laid bare all the little secrets of his

life ; she found out exactly why his tutor had refused him college testimonials ; there was nothing in his whole career, no youthful folly, that she did not hunt out. He could keep nothing from her.

'And you are really twenty-five, Stephen,' she said to him one day—she called him Stephen now—'and you have never, never been in love ?'

' No ; never seriously,' he answered with a laugh. ' I'm afraid I don't know what the genuine thing is.'

' No ? You have never met the right woman, or you would know,' she said softly. And then she sighed.

' I suppose not,' said Stephen, laughing. ' How should I know she was the right woman if I did meet her ?'

'Oh, you would know, Stephen. Your heart would tell you. You could not make a mistake.'

Again the Baroness sighed.

She had a very taking sigh—large women have.   It seemed to come up from very deep down, and it was of considerable volume.   It contained at least material for a dozen ordinary sighs.

Stephen hadn't the least idea what she was sighing for.

' What kind of women do you admire ? Do you like fair women or dark ?   Do you like a cold, phlegmatic woman, devoted to Sunday-schools and mothers' meetings, or a woman with a warm Southern nature, whose love you would never probe the depths of——'

Stephen didn't know what was coming, and he began to feel — not exactly cold shivers down his back—and he looked up, and caught a gleam in the golden-yellow eyes that were looking fondly down into his —he happened to be sitting on a low chair,

and the Baroness was on the couch beside
him—that he had never seen there before,
and it gave him that curious sensation down
his spine.

' I think I prefer the lady who would
look after the Sunday-schools, and take the
mothers' meetings,' he said promptly ; and
then he got up and went away.

It was quite time he went away.

His visits to the Hermitage had not
passed unnoticed in that gossiping, scandal-
loving community. Every tea - table in
Thorpe had for its chief topic the doings
of the worldly - minded curate that Mr.
Banister had unwisely selected. He ought
to have called a meeting of elderly spinsters
and laid the applications of the various
candidates before them, and they would
have selected a delightful young man after
their own heart. Some people went so far
as to say that Mrs. Banister had chosen

Stephen, that poor Mr. Tom was so hen-
pecked that he had no voice in the selec-
tion.

Mrs. Tom gave quite sufficient grounds
for the report. She took Stephen's part
in everything; she was loyal even in the
matter of the dancing.

'I hope you have got over your dis-
appointment about the dancing,' she said to
him one day when she thought he was
looking unusually gloomy, and she had an
idea that the failure of his pet scheme was
rankling in his mind. 'I should have liked
it myself, and I'm sure it wouldn't have done
the people any harm; see how they dance
in Italy and in France. I don't know that
we are any better for taking things so
gloomily; but, you see, it wouldn't have
done for Tom to take it up. There are a
lot of old women always waiting to find
fault. Oh, what a story they would have

made of it! They would have written to
the Bishop.'

'Yes,' Stephen admitted sadly; 'I suppose they would have found fault. They
find fault with most things; but I don't
think they are altogether to be considered.
I think we should take a higher stand than
public opinion.'

'Oh, I'm not a bit afraid of Mrs. Grundy
personally. Nothing gives me more pleasure
than to hear her squeal; but there is Tom
to consider, and the parish. I suppose it's
one's duty to live peaceably with one's flock,
not to set everybody's back up if one can
help it. Still, I wish it could have been
arranged.'

'It's a pity,' Stephen said; 'and I think
it's an opportunity lost. It isn't as if the
people didn't like it and didn't do it already.
At the fair last week there was dancing kept
up until daylight; and at Easter and Whit-

suntide there is always dancing at the public-houses. They do it secretly, as it were, and there is a good deal of drinking going on with it. If we could have made it a creditable and lawful amusement, there would have been no need for it to take place in the back-rooms of a public-house. If we had taken it up, it would immediately have become an innocent and quite decent and reputable recreation. Oh, I am sure we are doing wrong by putting our foot upon the amusements of the people. We pervert their moral sense. They *will* have amusement of some kind, and if we refuse them what is really innocent, we encourage them to seek for it in a baser form. I don't know why we should go out of our way to teach people that recreation is wicked ; we have no authority for it—certainly no Divine authority.'

' You should tell Tom all this ; it is

no use telling me,' the Rector's wife said.
' I think he wouldn't have raised any objec-
tion if Lady Camilla hadn't cooled. It would
have been her project, not his ; and she is
thought so much of here that people wouldn't
have dared to say anything.'

'We have got the room, at any rate. We
should not have got the room if it hadn't
been for the dancing. I don't know what
we should do without it, it is so useful for
lectures and meetings.'

'You have got more than the room,
Mr. Dashwood. You don't know what
you have got. A surveyor and an archi-
tect have been down, and Sir Probyn is
going to build some new cottages at Littlecourt. They are to be built with all the
latest sanitary improvements. It will be a
great boon to those poor creatures. When
you ask for one thing you often get another.
Providence, I suppose, knows what is best.'

Stephen couldn't but own, perhaps a little grudgingly, that Providence knew what was best. It certainly knew better than he did. He had asked for a dancing-booth, and it had given him a spacious, much-needed parish-room, and now it had put it into the heart of the most indifferent landlord in the county to build some model, quite model, cottages on his estate in the place of those horrible, unsanitary dwellings at Littlecourt that were not fit for pigs to live in.

They were not small things, they were really great things, he had to be thankful for. He was quite ashamed of himself for not being more thankful, for still hankering after the things that had been denied.

Perhaps the time was not ripe for them.

Stephen did not go to the Hermitage again for some time. When he did go he went a little earlier than usual, intending not to

stay late. He had come to think lately
that it would be much better for him to
go to the Hermitage earlier in the day
than was his wont—say to luncheon or tea,
five o'clock tea, and a little gossip ; to
any meal, in fact, except supper. That
taking off of armour—the spiritual armour,
that is always fraught with danger to take
off—at the end of the day, when the work
was over, and sitting down to feasting, and—
not exactly revelry—soft music and lowered
lights, was not exactly the kind of discipline
he needed. He didn't find it out until that
night when the Baroness asked that funny
question about the lady and the Sunday-
schools. Then, quite suddenly, he scented
danger. He found out, all at once, that
what he was accustomed to call sympathy
was 'spooning.' It is so much better to
call things by their right names.

This explained his calling earlier to-day.

He called so much earlier that nobody was expecting him. Bébée was dusting the drawing-room, and arranging some flowers in vases. She didn't do much arranging; she just stuck the flowers anyhow in the pots in a sulky, spiritless way. She looked as if she had been crying all day : her eyes were pinker than ever; her nose was very pink, and her face was white—quite white and colourless—and she wore a big white pinafore-apron that covered up her frock.

Stephen could not help remarking how exactly she resembled a white mouse as she stood beside the table sticking the flowers into the vases ; and then he noticed that her arms and hands were red, too— barred or striped with red—as if they had been torn by brambles. He could think of nothing else that could tear them in that way.

' Did you do that in getting the flowers ?' he asked.

Bébée looked up suddenly, and then he noticed what very green eyes she had— perhaps in contrast to the pink lids—and that her lips were quivering.

'It isn't that,' she said, glancing fearfully at the door ; '*she* set that brute at me again. Oh, how I wish I was dead !'

She left off sticking the flowers into the vases, and put her apron to her eyes, and Stephen thought she was going off into one of those fits of hysterics he had heard of.

' She ?' he repeated vaguely.

He was so taken aback by the girl's words that he didn't know what to say.

' Yes ; she's a tiger ! She isn't a woman. You can see it in her eyes. Did you ever see a woman with such eyes ? Her paws are velvet ; but, oh ! you should feel her claws. She has beaten me and pinched me so long as I can remember ; and now, when I tell tales about her, she sets that brute at me. It is not a cat; it is a tiger like herself.'

Clearly the girl was not accountable for what she said. Stephen tried to remember the tales he had heard about hysterical people saying the wildest things while the fit is on them.

Bébée was certainly hysterical. He expected to see her go off every moment into a laughing fit, or a crying fit, or both. He was very sorry, after all, that he had come so early. If he had come at the usual time, that Bluebeard cupboard he had just got a peep into would have been closed. He was sorry that the door had been left ajar for him to get that unpleasant glimpse within; he would have liked to have shut it softly and gone away.

'Poor pussy!' he said, with a dreary attempt at a laugh. 'I dare say she got the worst of it. I expect you were teasing her. Sit down, Bébée, and play one of those *Lieder* you are so fond of; it will calm your nerves.'

'I hate the piano, and I hate the ever-lasting *Lieder!* I wish Mendelssohn had never lived! I hate them all—Beethoven, or Bach, or Schumann, or Mozart—oh, how I hate them!'

The girl shuddered as she spoke, and a faint pink flush crept up under her white skin.

'Ah,' she went on in her rapid, excited way, and pausing every now and then to cast fearful glances in the direction of the door, 'you don't know what reason I have to hate them! She makes me play for hours and hours, until my fingers ache, and my back aches, and my eyes ache, and I get so giddy in my head that I can hardly keep from falling off the stool. If I stop without her permission, she beats me. She often

threatens me when you are sitting here
talking to her—she likes to hear you talk—
she speaks so soft, you do not guess what
she is saying.   Oh, if you only knew !'

The Baroness came into the room while
Bébée was speaking ; she had evidently
stayed to dress, and she was smoothing
down her laces as she came into the
room.

Something in the girl's face or manner
caught her eye as she came in smiling, with
her shapely white jewelled hand outstretched
to Stephen.

'What is the matter ? what are you
talking about, Bébée ?'

The great black cat had glided in beside
her, and it stood rubbing itself against the
table where the girl was standing.

Bébée had dropped her apron, and was
sullenly sticking the flowers in the vases
before her.

' I was telling Mr. Dashwood that I had
got my hands scratched with the brambles
in getting these horrid flowers,' she said
sullenly.

And then she gathered up the litter she
had made on the table, and took herself and
her litter out of the room.

Stephen felt exactly as if he had been
detected with the key of the Bluebeard
cupboard in his hand.

CHAPTER VI.

NAUSICAA.

THE curate of St. Michael's did not find out everything about his parish at once.

There were a great many places and people he had not visited when he had been in Thorpe Regis a year. He had called on most of the poor people, and he had visited the sick; there were a good many sick people in Thorpe. The lower end of the town, near the river, was damp and un-healthy, and if he had no other virtue, he was unfailing in his ministrations to the sick.

Perhaps for this reason Stephen got on better with his poorer parishioners than he did with the rich; they understood him better. He was more familiar with poor men's dwellings than with their wealthier neighbours. He saw more of them at those solemn seasons when pretences are laid aside, and they had learnt to speak to him unreservedly of their cares and fears for this world and the next. If he had accomplished nothing else during his first year of work in Thorpe, he was the sympathizing friend of every working man, woman, and child in the parish.

There were some outlying districts which he had not yet visited; he had quite enough to do to visit the people in the parish, without going out of his way to call upon people who lived outside it.

During all the year he had been in Thorpe, he had never found out Wellbrook Lane until one hot August noon, when, returning from a dusty walk along the

dreary, scorching highroad, he was tempted
to turn down the shady lane, that led
apparently to nowhere, out of the glare and
heat of the sun.

Then he made a discovery.

All precious things, we are told, are discovered late. If he had gone down Wellbrook Lane in the spring-time, he would
have found that not only primroses decked
the bank's green side, but violets, harebells,
daffodils, wood orchis, hyacinth—every sweet
thing of the copse or meadow—crowded up
here in its season, and that the air was
always fragrant with blossom and tuneful
with song. There was always a lark going
up or coming down in Wellbrook Lane, and
there was a brook, from which it took its
name, murmuring hard by.

The harebells and the wood orchis were
over now ; they had bloomed their short
windy day, and the hawthorns that had

whitened the hedges had gone too, and the sweet wild roses that had blushed in the July sun had faded, but the perfume of the honeysuckle was still sweet and strong, and the foxgloves were tall and brave, and the little speedwell's darling blue was everywhere reflecting back the blue, blue August sky.

Stephen thought he had never seen such a delightful country lane in his life.

Perhaps it was the relief of the coolness after the glare and heat of the dusty highway. He couldn't think why he hadn't found it out before.

He was sure that all this wealth of beauty was the prelude to something sweeter yet. He had no idea where this fairy glade led to ; he was sure he was on the verge of a discovery.

He might have been another fairy prince.

It used to be his favourite myth in those old wild days when he had differences with the college authorities. He always thought he should discover a sleeping princess. He certainly hadn't discovered one at the Hermitage. He had discovered a Blue-beard cupboard that he would rather have been ignorant of. The discovery had made his visits awkward. He always felt he was sharing a secret with Bébée, and he was positively afraid of the Baroness—and he hated the cats.

No ; the sleeping princess, that he was some day to awake, was not at the Hermitage.

He had often wondered what had become of that girl everybody said he was flirting with at Mrs. Tom's unlucky tennis-party. He had never seen her since that day ; he had forgotten even her name, and he had behaved so badly on that occasion that he hadn't dared to ask about her since.

She had disappeared as completely from Thorpe society as if some malignant fairy had caught her up, and whisked her a thousand miles away.

He was quite certain of one thing—she was not in Thorpe. He was thinking about her as he wandered idly down Wellbrook Lane. Something in the atmosphere of the place recalled her. Faint shadows from the branches overhead fell across his path—faint murmurs from the fields, where the corn was already ripening for the harvest, and whispering vague hints and echoes of the days to come.

Something of the mystery, the silence, and sweet, sweet sadness of the time and place stirred his blood, and brought back the face of the girl he had met for the last and first time on that well-remembered day. Perhaps it was the scent of the honeysuckle in the hedge that brought her back so

vividly. He remembered then, for the first
time, that she had some crimson - tipped
honeysuckle at her waist. She might have
gathered it from a trailing branch that grew
above his head. He made a leap and
caught it, and crushed it, as men crush
sweetness, in his hand, and in a moment the
whole scene was before him—Rectory, lawn,
and a rosebud garden of girls, and a girl on
the turf by his side, panting and pink—no,
scarlet—who was lily and rose in one.

A bit of honeysuckle had brought it all
back.

A wall of greenery and creeping plants had
shut out a house that lay back from the road
from his view. He did not see it till he
reached the gate, and then, as he stood
looking over the gate, he remembered he had
never seen the house before.

It was only a cottage, rather out of repair,
covered with creepers and parasites that

wanted fastening up dreadfully. There was
an ill-kept garden in front of the cottage,
and a gravelled path that was overgrown
with weeds. It had such a forlorn, neglected
look that, if it hadn't been for the smoke
that was curling up into the blue sky from
one of the chimneys, Stephen would have
thought it was uninhabited. Reassured by
the smoke, and remembering that he had
done no visiting this hot, idle summer day,
he opened the garden-gate and went up to
the door.

He went up quite boldly; he did not
pause or hesitate. He climbed the two
steps that led to the front-door as if they had
been one, and then he rapped boldly at the
door. There was no bell to the house, so
that he couldn't ring; and there was no
knocker, so he rapped at the door with the
knob of his stick. He rapped as boldly as
if it had been a door on a college staircase,

and he waited with the handle in his hand
ready to turn when the voice within shouted,
' Come in !'

But no one shouted, 'Come in!' and the
handle wouldn't turn.

He waited a few moments, and then he
rapped again a little louder and a more
imperative summons than before ; and then,
while he stood sunning himself on the doorsteps and noting all the signs of neglect and
decay about the place, somebody opened the
door.

He would have taken off his hat if he
had known it was a Girton girl who had
opened the door ; he ought to have taken it
off as it was ; and the vision that he saw—
the quite unexpected vision—dazzled him,
and he was rather sorry he had made such
a noise with that confounded stick.

He had only expected to find quite
ordinary working people living in this

gloomy little house, hiding away from the road, when he opened the garden-gate and went in.

The girl who answered his impatient summons didn't look the least like a Girton girl when she opened the door.

Stephen Dashwood was a little short-sighted, and this vision of a lovely young woman, with her sleeves turned up above her elbows—and very pretty elbows they were—and her skirts gathered up about her knees, and a big coarse apron tied round her waist, with a big coarse bib pinned under her chin, rather took away his breath. He couldn't be sure if it was the maid or the mistress he was speaking to, and he didn't at all expect to see a lady in Wellbrook Lane.

' I beg your pardon——' he said, and paused.

Something in the girl's eyes had stopped

that ready flow of words with which he
addressed himself to his humbler parishioners.

'Yes?' said the Girton girl, looking
straight at him, and holding the door wide
open, but not inviting him to walk in.

'I—I am afraid I haven't the pleasure of·
knowing the name. I have only recently
come to the parish.'

'No,' said the Girton girl.

She didn't at all attempt to help him
out.

'May I ask the name?' Stephen said
desperately.

'Grove,' said the girl—'Mary Grove.
Perhaps you'd like to see my mother?'

'I should like to see her very much, if
it's convenient—if I'm not intruding. Pray
don't let me interrupt you! Pray don't stop
your work for me! I can talk to you while
you are at work if you will allow me.'

'Just as you please,' said Mary Grove,
with just a suspicion of a smile about the
corners of her lips; 'I am washing, and
my mother is hanging out the clothes.
Perhaps you would like to talk to her in the
garden.'

She led the way through the passage to
the garden at the back of the house—a big
green garden, full of sunshine and homely
flowers. Some lines had been stretched
across between the apple-trees, and a frail-
looking, shabby little woman was hanging
out some linen.

'Mamma, this is Mr. Banister's new
curate,' Mary Grove said, introducing the
visitor; and then she retired to a bench that
stood outside the kitchen-door, with a tub
of steaming soap-suds upon it, and re-
commenced her washing.

Mrs. Grove put down her clothes-pegs,
and held out her hand to him; it was a

thin, wasted hand, and her face, he remarked, looked worn and sad. It was the face of a lady, and, faded and shabby as she looked in the morning sunshine, Stephen knew he was talking to a gentlewoman.

'I ought to have introduced myself to your daughter,' he said. 'My name is Dashwood — Stephen Dashwood. I have only lately come to Thorpe. I am trying to call upon everybody; I should have called before, but I have only just found out Wellbrook Lane.'

Mrs. Grove smiled.

'Few people find out Wellbrook Lane,' she said, just smothering a sigh.

'Then you have not many visitors?'

'We have no visitors.'

Stephen glanced unconsciously in the direction of the bench. Mary was bending over the wash-tub, and she was singing at her work. She had forgotten all about

him already; she was deep in soapsuds,
and singing a sweet low cradle-song :

'Sweet and low, sweet and low.'

Sweet, sweet, sweet! he had never heard
any sound so sweet in his life, and he had
never seen such a comely pair of ankles ;
and the profile that was bending over the
wash-tub might have been the profile of
Nausicaa herself. Looking at Mary Grove,
standing there at the wash-tub in the sweet
morning sunshine, he recalled Homer's
idyllic episode of Alcinous' daughter going
washing with her maidens.

Washing clothes was not considered un-
refined in those old simple days, and a
king's daughter could go down with her
maidens to the stream and wash the clothes
of the household ; and a poet too refined to
see anything mean or ridiculous in healthy
natural labour immortalizes the idyllic scene
in his noble verse.

Mrs. Grove followed the direction of Stephen's eyes, and sighed. She knew nothing about Nausicaa. She had never read a line of Homer in her life. Girls did not go up to Girton in her days.

'You are thinking it is dull for Mary,' she said. 'I think not. She would not like to see any visitors now;' and then the tears came into her eyes, and she broke down.

'I am afraid you are in trouble,' said the curate gently ; and he laid his hand on the thin, worn hand that was still grasping the clothes-pegs. It was but a light touch— a mere feather-weight—but it broke down all her reticence, and her tears flowed freely. She was not used to sympathy.

'Is it possible you have not heard ?' she said.

'No; I have heard nothing. I have come here so lately. I am a stranger to

the place and the people. If you will tell
me your trouble I shall be very glad to help
you, to be of service to you in any way I
can ;' and again he glanced at Nausicaa,
though, as her back was turned to him, he
only caught a glimpse of her ankles.

The poor woman looked at Stephen
through her tears. It was a kind face, if
not a strong face. It was a face that a
woman couldn't help trusting.

And sitting there on the garden-bench,
with a basket of wet linen at her feet, and
her hands full of clothes-pegs, Mrs. Grove
told him her story.

A sad little story of sorrow and loss and
endurance and heroism.

It was very commonplace heroism ; it was
the endurance that is practised every day of
their lives by thousands of women ; it was
the old, old story of trial and loss. There
was nothing in the story itself remarkable ;

it was exactly like the story that thousands
of women could tell, and are telling daily,
until the world gets tired of listening to
them.   Stephen, hearing it from Mrs. Grove's
lips as he sat in the shade of the apple-trees,
with the basket of wet linen that Mary
Grove had just washed at his feet, thought
it the saddest story he had ever heard ; it
brought the tears smarting into his eyes.

Mary Grove's father was a drunkard.

He had been a major in the army, and
he was a major now only in name.   He had
sold out years ago.   He had parted with a
great many other things besides his com-
mission.   House and lands, and furniture
and plate—everything that could be turned
into money had gone.   It had all gone one
way.

He had drunk it all.

Lower and lower he had sunk year by
year, dragging his family with him into the

dust, and now there was nothing left but the dwindling interest of a small freehold that had been his wife's jointure.

There were two girls—only girls—no boys to drag down with him to this low level. It would have been dreadful to a boy, this slipping down, down, down! It was bad enough to girls. One girl had got out of it; she was a teacher in a foreign boarding-school, and she was blissfully ignorant of the low level that had already been reached. What was the use of telling her? The other girl was a student of a woman's college. She had won a scholarship, and a maiden aunt had left her a small legacy, and with these slender means she had gone to Girton.

Everything was slipping away—every-thing here: it would soon be all gone; but what she gained at Girton—and she had already gained, oh, so much!—was beyond the reach of loss or accident. If she took a First Class she would be able to look the future in the face without fear or dismay; she would be quite prepared for that black day she saw so surely coming.

The black day came sooner than she expected. It came when her three years' work at Girton—it had been very hard work; nobody but herself knew how hard —was drawing to a close; when success, so hardly earned, was assured. It would not be delayed a single day; if it could have been delayed a single term she would have been prepared to meet it.

Year by year everything had been going from bad to worse, and now the worst had been reached. Major Grove had had a dreadful fit of delirium tremens, and the doctor who attended him had said that a recurrence of the attack was inevitable, and that the dear, patient woman who had clung to him with uncomplaining love and fidelity through all these unhappy years ran a daily, hourly risk of her life.

Mary Grove threw up Girton and her First Class, and stayed at home with her mother.

She was doing the washing now, outside the kitchen-door, and she was singing at her work. She had already resigned herself to her lot; undertaken her dreary *métier* practically, if not pathetically, without the least cynicism or tragedy airs.

Stephen listened to the little sad story with a white, set face and tightening lips, and when she came to the end—to that last sad chapter, to the crowning sacrifice, Mary's refusal to go back to Girton — the tears rushed into his eyes, and he covered his face with his hands. He was a dreadfully emotional, highly-strung young man, and he couldn't control himself.

' It was against my wish she stayed,' Mrs. Grove was saying ; ' I could have borne it for three months longer. I *would* have borne it. I would have suffered anything for Mary to have gone up this last term, to have gone in for the examination she had been working so hard for. She would have taken a high place, I am told——'

' I am sure she would !' said Stephen hotly.

What did he know about it ?

' Miss English, the Principal, wrote and offered to forego the fees if she would go up for the examination. They had counted so much upon her at Girton ; it was a great disappointment. I think they expected she would take a First Class.'

' Of course she would take a First !' said Stephen warmly. He was quite as certain of it as if he had been one of the examiners, and had the papers before him.

'Nothing would persuade Mary to go back,' continued Mrs. Grove, fondly smoothing down the wooden pegs in her lap ; 'she would not hear of it. She would not leave me alone with him again ; she is so careful for me, and so indifferent for herself, and— and, in spite of all, she really loves her father. No one can manage him as she does when he is really violent, and he is very violent at times. I sometimes think he will kill her, but she is never afraid. She is so brave, and so tender and patient. It breaks my heart to see her doing this work, but she will not have a woman in to do it. She will not let any stranger come in to see our trouble. It is a dreadful, a shameful, sight at times, and she cannot bear that anyone should come in and see it. Oh, no one knows what she has to go through ! My poor child !'

Stephen could stand it no longer ; he got

up from the garden-seat, and walked backward and forward across the lawn, with the
wet clothes on the line flapping against his
face.

Once, and once only, he glanced over to
Nausicaa, who was singing at her work,
and caught a glimpse of the bright chestnut
hair, and the lovely profile, and the dainty
curve of the dainty neck, and the sweep of
the handsome shoulders bending over the
wash-tub.   He was so moved, so infatuated,
with this bit of humble heroism, with this
Girton girl who had formed for herself such
a high and pure ideal of duty in the most
commonplace surroundings, in this menial
occupation, that he likened her in his
emotional mind to the heroes of old—the
true, simple old heroes—who were kinsmen
of the gods.

He would have liked to have fallen down
at her feet beside the wash - tub, and

worshipped her, as he worshipped, rightly or wrongly, the saintly women of old, who, in their infinite sense of duty, raised the ideal of human nobleness.

How could he help this girl? he asked himself, as he walked backward and forward among the wet clothes.

'Would it be any use my seeing Mr.— Major Grove?' he asked presently, stopping before the garden-seat.

'I don't think it would be any use,' the poor woman said with a sigh. 'He is past seeing anyone. He would be very angry if anyone were brought in, and—and he might insult you. He forgets sometimes that he is a gentleman. He might be violent and use dreadful language. No; I don't think you can see him.'

Stephen groaned inwardly. The man was too dreadful for him to see, and this girl had to endure it day and night—the coarseness, and the violence, and the dreadful language!

'I shouldn't mind his being angry,' he said, 'if I can do him any good. Where is he now?'

'Oh, he is not up yet! He never comes down till the afternoon. The morning is our only happy time. Mary ought to be lying down now; she was up all night, and if he is violent again to-night, she will not dare' to go to bed until morning. He generally gets quieter towards morning.'

'I will come again, if you will let me, Mrs. Grove,' Stephen said, as he took his leave. 'I should like to help you if I can— if you will let me try.'

'It is very kind of you,' said the poor little woman sadly; 'but we see no one now. I don't think we can trespass upon your time——'

'It isn't *my* time,' interrupted Stephen,

with a look in his eyes that Mrs. Grove
hadn't seen there before ; 'it's my Master's
time. I don't think the age of miracles
has passed. Will you let me try, Mrs.
Grove ?'

'You must ask Mary. If she thinks that
you can do any good, come — come by
all means, and God bless you for coming!'

It was one thing to say, 'Ask Mary,' and
another thing to ask her.

Stephen Dashwood approached Mary
Grove with his heart beating dreadfully, and
the tell-tale colour in his face ; but the white-
armed Nausicaa did not look up until he
paused beside the wash-tub.

'You have had a long talk with my
mother,' she said, smiling across the tub ;
but she did not leave off her everlasting rub-
rub, scrub-scrub.

She was not the least ashamed of her
dress or her occupation. She was as cool

and composed as if she were in the lecture-
room at Girton.

' Yes,' he said gravely ; ' she has been
telling me about her great trial. She has
taken me into her confidence—I hope you
will not think it misplaced—and she has
promised, with your consent, to let me help
her.'

' With my consent ?' Mary repeated ; and
she paused in her work, and the blood
rushed up into her face. ' Has she told you
all—all ?'

' She has told me all.'

Mary took her hands out of the water ;
she didn't wipe them on her apron as a
washerwoman should have done, but she
stood with them hanging down by her side,
with the soapy water dripping off her slender
fingers and her white arms, and the sunshine shining on the soap - bubbles, and
irradiating them with the most glorious

prismatic colours, till they shone like rubies,
and sapphires, and opals, and diamonds—
living jewels coming and going in the sun-
light.

'You know all--everything; and—and
you think you can help us?'

'I know everything, and I am sure I can
help you.'

His tone was confident, and his lips were
firm and strong, and his eyes were shining.

Mary measured him with one quick,
searching glance. She had not spent three
years at Girton for nothing. She was quick
to perceive the character of this Ulysses
who had interrupted her washing — this
champion who was eager to fight her battles
for her.

'If you can help us, we shall be very
grateful,' she said softly; and he saw that
her lip trembled as she spoke.

'When may I come?' he said eagerly—

'when may I begin? May I come to-night
—to-morrow?'

She smiled at his eagerness; she did not
know what tales her mother had been telling him about her having been up all the
night before, and what she would have to
go through again to-night.

'Come to-morrow,' she said — 'come in
the afternoon;' and then, with her jewelled
arms still dripping, she took him back
through the house, and opened the front-
door to let him out.

'My hands are wet,' she said, smiling, and
drawing back when he would have shaken
hands with her at the door.

He shook hands, nevertheless, and his
hands were tingling with that warm, damp
touch all the way back to Thorpe.

CHAPTER VII.

ST. HELENA.

IF staying at home and doing one's duty is a form of heroism, Mary Grove was a heroine.

If she had stayed at Girton and taken her First Class, she would certainly have been a heroine—the world would not have disputed her claim—but to stay at home, and take care of a drunken old father and a poor broken-hearted mother, it really seemed such a common-place thing that it was no wonder the people of Thorpe Regis saw nothing heroic in it.

It is so hard to define heroism. There

is no fixed standard. It is not duty, though it is its perfect fulfilment. It goes beyond duty ; it is a work of supererogation.

There are heroines—the world is full of them—who neglect every duty. It is so much easier to step out of one's sphere to do some big thing, with the world looking on and applauding, than to do the mean, troublesome, disagreeable little duties that hang like a millstone about one's neck.

Perhaps that is where the heroism comes in. The big thing may be, after all, the result of pride, self-will, discontent, emulation ; and the true hero or heroine stays at home and does the humble work, and is never heard of.

Who shall say ?

It is only fair to Mary Grove to say that it never entered into her head that she was doing anything unusual—anything beyond her duty. She stayed at home, and threw up her First Class, and accepted her humble lot cheerfully.

It was a hard, ungracious lot, as well as a humble one. Everything had slipped away, and it was a hard struggle to eke out the little slender income that had been saved out of the wreck.

This accounted for the poor cottage, and the neglected garden, and the wash-tub outside the kitchen door.

Wellbrook Lane was so far away from the town, and the place was in such a dilapidated condition, that the rent was low, and there were no neighbours to spy out the nakedness of the land.

Mary Grove never could be thankful enough that Wellbrook Lane was not in the town. There might have been houses on either side if it had been a street, and there would have been neighbours always listening and hearing those dreadful, dreadful noises.

Fortunately the house lay well back from the road, and the Major could scream and swear to his heart's content without disturbing anybody. He raved and swore all day now, and the two trembling women kept the windows and doors that looked out on the road close shut, vainly trying to cover up their shame and misery.

There really was no need to keep the front-door so carefully closed against the world, for no one ever called in Wellbrook Lane now. People did not care to run the risk of encountering a drunken, raving madman. There could be no question of social intercourse, so Mrs. Grove and her daughter dropped out of Thorpe society. Mary Grove was very glad to have it so. Not a soul, except the butcher and the baker and the milkman, had called at the house since

she had come back from Girton in March,
and now it was August, until that day when
Stephen found her out.

He hadn't found her out a minute too
soon.

He couldn't get that picture of the Girton
girl at the wash-tub out of his mind—out
of his sight, indeed—do what he would, all
that day.

He could see her quite plainly, every time
he shut his eyes, standing in the sunshine,
with her arms bare and her skirts gathered
up, bending over the steaming tub.   He
could see the beautiful profile, and the pose
of the stately head, rising like a flower on
a stalk.   He saw it all quite plainly ; he
even recalled a dimple that he had seen but
one second, when she smiled at him across
the wash-tub ; and all about her was a subtle
atmosphere like the cloud-like atmosphere
of the gods—it might have been steam.

He drew the picture from memory, steam and all, only he idealized it as clouds—clouds about her feet and about her head, and angels—little fat, chubby angels, that looked very much like Cupids—perched on the clouds, and looking down upon her.

Then it occurred to him that he had seen a picture somewhere exactly like it—a picture by an old Master, Raphael or Paul Veronese—a kind of St. Helena at the wash-tub, with angels watching her.

No; it wasn't St. Helena.

Where had he seen it?

Perhaps in a stained-glass window at Cambridge—one of the wonderful windows at King's College Chapel. He remembered them all. Hadn't he sat under them, and looked up at them, term after term, for three years, and puzzled them painfully out bit by bit, making many mistakes, and going over them again and again? He knew them all by heart at last, every one of them, and, maybe, had learnt some of the lessons they taught. He couldn't sit under them for three years without learning something.

He recalled them all, type and anti-type, but he couldn't recall a woman at a washing-tub among them. Then he turned over his lives of the saints with the same result. He lingered over them lovingly—he was very fond of the saints—St. Dorothy with her flowers, St. Barbara with her tower, St. Gertrude with her loaf, St. Faith with her rods, St. Margaret trampling on the dragon, St. Catherine and her wheel: no, there wasn't a wash-tub among them.

Clearly, if Mary Grove were put into a church-window, the Archbishop of Canterbury would have to canonize a new saint.

Well, he might go farther for a saintly ideal of heroism than the Girton girl at the wash-tub.

Stephen talked the matter over with his

Rector the same evening. He found
Banister smoking his post-prandial pipe in
the Rectory garden among the flower-beds.
Mrs. Tom had gone up to the nursery to
hear Tommy and Poppy say their evening
prayers, and the Rector was alone.

'I have made a discovery,' Stephen began,
trying to keep his voice steady, and looking
down at the gravel path ; 'I have found out
a new parishioner. I have been in Wellbrook Lane.'

The Rector stopped in the middle of the
path.

'You don't mean to say you have called
upon the Groves ?' he said in a tone of
positive alarm.

'I have indeed ; why shouldn't I call ?
They are quite within the boundary of the
parish.'

'It isn't that, but the circumstances are
peculiar—I might say embarrassing.'

'So I should suppose, but that wouldn't
have prevented my calling, even if I had
known it ; but I didn't know it when I
knocked at the door. I expected to find
labouring people.'

' Who did you see ?'

' I saw Miss Grove. She opened the door
to me.'

' Mary ? Poor girl ! So she let you in ?
She doesn't let many people in. She won't
let my wife in very often, though she's the
only friend she has in the place ; and she
won't let me in when the Major's violent.
She always sends a message out by the
girl that he isn't well enough to see anyone.'

' I didn't see him, but I'm going to see
him to-morrow.'

' I don't think you will. The women
won't let anyone see him. I don't wonder
at it. It must be a shameful spectacle. He

is never sober, I hear, and he leads them a
terrible life. He spends every penny he has
got in the world on drink. One can't blame
them for refusing to see anyone. It must be
hard enough to bear without the shame of it,
and the exposure.'

' They are going to let me see him to-
morrow : Mrs. Grove has promised me, and
Mary—Miss Grove—has given her consent.'

' I can't understand it ; I think you must
have charmed them, Dashwood ;' and the
Rector paused in his walk and looked
straight in his curate's face.

There was really no reason why Stephen
should blush like a girl. He had only been
doing his duty. He had only paid a purely
parochial visit to a shabby old woman who
was hanging out the clothes.

' Well,' said the Rector good-humouredly,
with a twinkle in his eyes—he had drawn

his own conclusions from that ridiculous poppy colour in his curate's face—' well, and what was Mary doing? Was she deep in moral science?'

'She was washing.'

'Washing! What do you mean? Did you surprise her at her toilet?'

'She was washing clothes—linen—at a wash-tub, and her mother was hanging it out on a line to dry.'

'Mary Grove washing! Why, do you know what she is, Dashwood? She is a Girton girl. She has done splendidly in Cambridge. She has taken a First in every exam. she has gone into, and she was safe for a First in her Tripos, if this old rascal of a father of hers hadn't broken out, and kept her at home out of sheer terror for what he might do, and for what he may at any moment do, to that poor, long-suffering woman.'

'You don't mean that you think that they—that Mrs. Grove is in actual bodily danger?' Stephen said, turning quite white at the bare suggestion.

'I do indeed. I shouldn't be the least surprised any morning to hear that he had murdered one or both of the women in the night. He is always worse of nights.'

'Good heavens! And can no one interfere?'

'I don't see that they can. The man isn't mad. He's as sane as you and I are in his sober moments. No one has any right to interfere. So long as the women don't complain and ask for protection from a justice of the peace, no one can interfere.'

'Not if he murders them in their beds?'

'No; not if he murders them in their beds. Not unless they happen to cry out, and open their door for the police to come in; they have no right to break in, whatever

they may hear going on inside. An
Englishman's house is his castle, you know.'

' And he has the right to bully and beat
the helpless women about him whenever he
likes ?' Stephen said bitterly.

' Exactly ; he has a perfect right. The
law cannot interfere unless a complaint is laid
before a magistrate, or some definite charge
is made. A man has a right to frighten and
beat his womenkind to death, stopping short
at actual murder, and the law cannot interfere. If he were out of his mind, it would
be another thing ; but he is not out of his
mind—at least, the doctors say he is sane,
and able to manage his own affairs, although
I have my own opinion on that point.'

' You think he is mad ?'

' Undoubtedly. Whatever he may be
physically, morally he is not answerable for
anything that he may do or say. He is as
mad as any lunatic tied up in a strait-

jacket in the county asylum. I am not sure
that a strait-jacket would not be the best
thing for him.'

'Does Mary—Mrs. Grove—know anything of this?'

'She may; she must guess it. She
cannot go on witnessing the scenes she does
witness, and know that this is not the same
man who, a dozen years ago, was one of the
most polished gentlemen in the county.
The worst of it is, she shuts herself out
from the world –she will not see anyone if
they call upon her — and then, poor soul!
she fancies that everybody has heard her
story, and that people look down upon her
because she has fallen in the world and is
tied to a drunken husband.'

'Poor soul!' said Stephen; but he was
thinking of the daughter, not of the mother.
He was very sorry for the poor lady who
suffered in silence, but his heart was full to

bursting for the sufferings of that sweet soul
who bent her meek face—no; it was not a
meek face—who bowed her meek shoulders
over the washing-tub.

He had the picture before his eyes the
next day, when he knocked at the door of
the little house in Wellbrook Lane. He
quite expected to see Mary open the door,
as he had seen her open it the day before,
with her arms bare, and her skirts gathered
up, and with a subtle aroma of soapsuds
surrounding her.

He was conscious of a feeling of dis-
appointment not to say disillusion, when the
door was opened by a maid-servant in a
spotless white apron and conventional cap.
It was an undersized maid-servant; the most
had been made of her years by gathering
her hair up in a knot behind beneath her
cap and lengthening her skirts. If it hadn't
been for her long frock, and the funny little

knot of hair behind, one would have doubted the vigilance of the Board school inspector.

She dropped Stephen a little curtsey, and took him into an inner room that looked out into the garden. He had time enough, when she had shut the door behind her, to take a hasty survey of the room before Mrs. Grove entered.

It was a wee back room, and it led out by a glass door into the garden. Meagre and bare and poor as it was, it was a lady's room. There were few signs of feminine occupation ; there was no fancy work—no antimacassars, or lace things, or china ornaments, or dainty chairs, or five o'clock tea-tables, or brackets. There was a little old-fashioned writing-bureau, like they use at Girton, with some papers scattered about, as if someone had just risen from it ; and above it was a small bookshelf—a lady's bookshelf — of well-used scholastic books.

Stephen glanced through them, as he stood there hat in hand, and he traced Mary Grove's University progress by them. Classics and mathematics on the top shelves, the authors she had read, and the cribs she had used, and the dictionaries that had assisted her—the smaller Smith, and the little Liddell and Scott; she had had to make the most she could of these modest helps. They had done more for her than big quartos do for some University students —they had helped her into the First Class of the ' Previous.'

On the lower shelf were the German books she had used in her Additionals ; and below, on the lowest shelf, were the moral science books that she had read for her Tripos.

Stephen turned away from that tale-telling bookshelf with a sigh. He didn't know how sorry he was for Mary Grove until he had seen that mute witness of her self-sacrifice. He remembered how eagerly he had looked forward to his own Tripos, and he knew exactly how she felt.

There were one or two photographs on the walls, all telling their own tale. One of King's College Chapel, another of the long avenue of Trinity, the world-famous bridge of St. John's, and the willows and sloping meadows of the Backs.

Stephen knew and loved them all, as every Cambridge man loves them. He had seen the originals thousands of times, but they had never stirred his pulse before ; but now the sight of them in this poor room, amid such surroundings, brought a mist before his eyes.

He was still looking at them when Mary Grove entered the room.

She came in through the glass door from the garden. She came in so softly that she surprised him looking at the pictures, and he turned round, confused and bewildered, with those foolish tears in his eyes, as if he had been detected in a guilty act. He hardly knew her for a moment. He couldn't recognise, until she spoke to him, the girl in the gray gown, that really touched the ground, and the tight-fitting bodice with sleeves that reached to the wrist, for the white-armed, short-skirted Nausicaa of yesterday. Of course Mary Grove could not always be washing; it must come to an end sometimes.

It was the same, but not the same.

Nausicaa shorn of her wash-tub and her jewelled arms; St. Helena without the clouds and the Cupids.

She looked taller and statelier, and decidedly graver; perhaps that was because her hair wasn't blowing about all over her face, and her petticoats were not tucked up.

Her face was a little flushed, and her eyes were harder and brighter than when Stephen last saw her bending over the wash-tub.

' I did not think you would come so early, Mr. Dashwood,' she said.

Was it his fancy, or was her voice harder and sharper, like her eyes?

' Have I come too soon?' he said, smiling, and making an utterly futile effort to hide his tears—his foolish tears.

' Papa is only just up,' said Miss Grove in her hard, forced voice, 'and—and he is worse than usual to-day. I don't think you can see him.'

Stephen's face fell.

' Is he more violent than usual, or is he really ill?' he asked, with just a perceptible quiver in his voice.

He was so anxious to help this girl; he was so afraid, so dreadfully afraid, what might happen if he didn't interfere at once, that he couldn't keep that quiver of dis-appointment out of his voice.

'I am afraid he is not well enough to see strangers,' she answered in her strained, forced voice, not looking at him, but looking out in the garden with a hard misery in her eyes that went to Stephen's heart. 'He has had a bad night ; we have been up all night with him, and—and he is only just up. He is not in a fit state to see anybody.'

'Is—is he——'

His lips wouldn't frame the question. He was ashamed of himself, and hung his head. What right had he to shame her with such a question ?

'Yes,' she said impatiently : 'he is—he is never sober. He is mad—quite mad! he *cannot* know what he is saying. He is very violent this morning ; he is saying at this moment the most dreadful things, and—and

I am afraid mamma is not safe to be left alone with him. If you'll excuse me, Mr. Dashwood, I think I must go——'

Even as she spoke there came a cry for help from a room at the other end of the passage. Mary Grove opened the door and fled down the passage, and Stephen followed her.

He followed her to the door of the room, and there he waited while the girl went in.

She threw back the door in her fright, and he could see all that was happening inside the room as he stood at the door. There was a fire burning in the grate, although it was full summer, and a couch was drawn up beside the fireplace. Mrs. Grove was bending over a prostrate figure on the floor when Mary rushed into the room. The Major had fallen down in his efforts to rise from the couch, and the two women were trying vainly to raise him.

Stephen didn't pause to consider whether

he was wanted or not. He strode into the room, and, putting the women aside, he picked up the prostrate figure, and laid him gently on the couch.

'I don't think he is much hurt,' he said as he laid him back on the couch.

There was no need for him to loosen his collar or undo his necktie; Major Grove had made his toilet without these adjuncts. He hadn't even thought it necessary to shave this morning, nor, apparently, for many mornings.

There was a grizzly beard of several days' growth on his chin, and his hair, which was iron-gray and wanted cutting dreadfully, was unkempt and falling low over his forehead.

His unshaven face, and his untidy dress, and his heavy breathing, told their miserable tale. He had been a handsome man once, but he was a wreck now –a complete wreck. If it had ever been a good face, or an intellectual face, or a kind face, it was none of these now.

Whatever beauty, or goodness, or intellect there had ever been in it had dropped out of it.   It was a coarse, soddened, flabby face, with swollen, discoloured features, and great dark, loose bags under the eyes.

It had drink—drink—drink—written-branded, rather — on every feature.   The image of the heavenly, if it had ever been there, was quite effaced, and it was stamped in ineffaceable characters with the image of the earthy.   At least, this was what Stephen Dashwood thought, as he stood beside the couch, looking down upon Mary Grove's father.   He tried in vain to trace any resemblance between the drink-soddened face on the pillow and the white, set face of the girl bending over him.

The Major was quite drunk, hopelessly drunk at that early hour of the day, and he

lay back on the couch in a deep sleep,
breathing heavily. Clearly nothing could
be done with him to-day. It was no use
talking to a man in that state.

Stephen said a few words to Mrs. Grove,
and then Mary beckoned him out of the
room. He left the poor lady standing
beside the couch wringing her hands. She
had wrung them, doubtless, hundreds of
times before, and she was wringing them
still in her dumb, dreadful agony. There
was nothing else left for her to do.

Stephen followed Mary Grove back to the
little room he had left, not exactly wringing
his hands, but clasping them tightly together
in a way that he had when he was very much
moved. It looked like a devotional attitude,
but it was only his way of repressing his
feelings. They wanted repressing very
often, and he had found this way of clasping his hands very effectual.

He was so ashamed of the spectacle he had just witnessed that he could not look at the girl before him when she had led him into the room and shut the door.

It seemed to him that the shame was his own, not hers.

'You have seen him,' she said, speaking breathlessly, 'and you know what he is exactly. Do you still think that—that anything can be done?'

'Ye-e-s,' said Stephen slowly, 'I still think that something can be done;' but he didn't say it very confidently.

'In what way?' said the girl impatiently. 'Oh, if you could only tell me in what way! We have tried everything—everything.'

'Yes, I am sure you have. You have had a doctor, of course; what doctor has he had?'

'None lately; he will not hear of a doctor. He drove Dr. Merivale out of the house.

He shut the door in his face because he told
him the truth.'

'I think he should see a doctor, whether
he is willing or not. I think—I may be
wrong—that it is a case that only a doctor
can deal with. It seems to me, judging
from what I have seen, that he cannot
control himself, and—and I am afraid you
have no control over him.'

'No,' said the girl bitterly; 'we have no
control over him—none.'

She stood in her white wretchedness dry-
eyed, looking out into the little green
garden, and Stephen stood silent and
ashamed beside her. He had promised to
help her, and he could do nothing but
suggest a doctor. He would have given
anything to help her if he only knew how.

'Will you let Dr. Merivale see him if I
fetch him now? It cannot matter to him
in his present state who sees him; he will

not recognise him, and if he should, the fact
of his falling down in a fit—it really is a kind
of fit—is a sufficient reason for sending for
medical aid.'

'You think it is a fit?' Mary asked
eagerly. 'He has fallen down suddenly
two or three times lately, and lain uncon-
scious, like he now is, sometimes for hours
after, and when he awakes he is bewildered,
and does not seem to know us.'

' I am sure it is a fit. Something serious
might happen—I do not say it will, but it
might at any moment—and he might not
recover consciousness. I think Mrs. Grove
should send for a doctor.'

Stephen did not leave the house until he
had wrung an unwilling consent from Mary
Grove to let him tell Dr. Merivale to call
in.

CHAPTER VIII.

MAD AS A HATTER.

IT was not until the day following that
Stephen heard the result of Dr. Merivale's
visit. Major Grove had recovered consciousness before the doctor arrived, and the
interview hadn't been a pleasant one.

He resented the doctor's interference ; he
refused to answer his questions ; and—well,
he didn't exactly insult him—he remembered, which fact he very often forgot when
he was alone with his womenfolk, that he
was a gentleman—but he let him understand
that his visit was unacceptable.

The next morning, before it was time for

the doctor to start upon his rounds, a letter was brought to him from Wellbrook Lane, stating that Major Grove had quite re- covered from his slight attack—he called it a slight attack — and that he would not trouble Dr. Merivale to call again. The letter was in Mary Grove's handwriting, and it was evidently written at the Major's dictation.

'Well,' said Stephen, when he had perused the precious epistle, 'and what are you going to do?'

'Do?' replied the doctor; 'do nothing. What can I do? I have received my dis- missal; I can only wait until some tragedy occurs—until he cuts his own throat or some- body else's.'

'You don't mean you are going to leave him in that state? Think of those help- less women, and the life he is leading them!'

'My dear fellow, what can I do? I can't attend a man against his will.'

'You could lock him up in an asylum. You say he is not responsible for what may happen. You could put him away where he would be looked after, and he couldn't do any injury to those dear women.'

'Ah, I see you don't know anything about the lunacy laws! A man may murder a houseful of people, but nobody can interfere until after the event, and then it isn't generally very much use.'

'But he is quite mad.'

'He is as mad as a hatter!'

'And you can do nothing?'

'Nothing!'

Stephen had to rest satisfied with Dr. Merivale's report. He had to reconcile himself to the thought that the madman in Wellbrook Lane could murder those two dear women—he always spoke of them to himself as those 'dear women,' not 'dear sisters'—and no one could interfere to prevent him.

He could do exactly as he liked with his own ; he could ill-treat and torture them to any extent up to positive murder ; he could bully them to his heart's content ; he could make their days and nights miserable, almost unbearable ; he could make their lives a very—well, the reverse of a paradise upon earth, and no one could interfere.

The law distinctly refused to interfere. After a tragedy had occurred it would be time for the law to step in.

Stephen drew gruesome pictures of the situation all through that day—it was quite gruesome enough without any deepening of the shadows—and in the afternoon he could contain himself no longer ; he went boldly up to the door of Wellbrook Cottage and inquired for Mary Grove.

The small servant-maid opened the door, and admitted him unwillingly. She thought the ladies were engaged, but she would go and see.

Stephen didn't give her an opportunity to go and see. He followed her to the door of the little room where Mary Grove kept her books, and where were those well-remembered pictures of Cambridge.

Mary Grove was not engaged—at least, she was only writing a letter. She rose up from the table where she was writing when Stephen came in, and he noticed that her face was paler than he had yet seen it, and that there were dark circles beneath her eyes.

He took her hand silently. What could he say? He was thankful she wasn't murdered. He was quite sure she had been up all the previous night, and very likely she was going to sit up again to-night.

She saw the concern in his tell-tale face, and she smiled—a weak little wintry smile—and then the tears came into her eyes, and she broke down.

'It is nothing!' she said impatiently, almost fiercely, as he murmured some stupid platitudes.

He really didn't know what to say to her.

He could say the nicest possible things to the poor people in the parish when he visited them in trouble and bereavement. He had a special gift of sympathy; he could speak soothing words to the sick, and he could comfort the bereaved, and cheer the sorrowful; he could enter into all their griefs, and had a special message for each, but he had no message for Mary Grove.

It was not exactly a parochial visit.

'I have had bad news,' she explained presently—'at least, unexpected news, and it has upset me.'

' I am very sorry,' he said awkwardly, but he meant it.

' It is nothing to be sorry about,' said Mary Grove, smiling through her tears. ' My sister is coming home from Germany; she is the dearest girl in the world, and I ought not to be sorry that she is coming, only the news was so unexpected, and she is coming so suddenly there is no time to —to explain anything.'

' When is she coming ?'

' She is coming to-morrow—perhaps to-night.'

' So soon ?   And you did not at all expect her ?'

He really didn't know what else to say.

' Not the least.   She was getting on so well when we last heard.   She was at a school in Dresden—quite a big school, almost a college—and she taught English to the German girls.   She was very much

liked—no one could help liking Doll; the
girls used to rave about her.'

'Why is she coming home so suddenly?'

Mary Grove's face clouded.

'That is what I am anxious about,' she
said. 'I cannot understand it. We had a
letter from Doll only two days ago—a bright,
chatty letter, full of her plans for the summer
—and now, this morning, we have a letter to
say that she is on the road to England, that
she will be with us almost as soon as her
letter reaches us.'

'And she gives no explanation?'

'None; only a few hastily scribbled lines.
Oh, I hope nothing wrong has happened! I
hope she has not been sent home in disgrace!'

'What could have happened?'

'I don't know. I can't think what she
can have done. She was always doing wild
things, and getting into scrapes, when she

was at school in England ; but since she
has been in Germany she has been steadier,
and we have had such good accounts of
her.'

'Why should she have done anything ?
She may be coming home to—to be married,'
Stephen suggested in as sanguine a tone as
he could manage.

Mary Grove shook her head.

'No—o,' she said slowly ; 'I don't think
Doll is going to be married.'

'Why shouldn't your sister be going to be
married ?' he asked brusquely.

Mary smiled up into his face and shook
her head.

'No,' she said decidedly, 'Doll isn't the
kind of girl to get married off-hand in that
way. Doll will take a great deal of
marrying—I mean a great deal of prepara-
tions beforehand. I am afraid there is
something wrong. I am so anxious for

mother's sake. Poor mother! she has so much to trouble her already, and if anything went wrong with Doll it would break her heart.'

Then Stephen suddenly remembered he had come to inquire after the Major. He had forgotten all about him while they had been talking about Mary Grove's sister.

As he had surmised, Mary had been up all night. The Major had been unusually violent; the doctor's visit had 'upset' him, and he had kept the little household up all night, and in the morning he had made Mary write that letter to Dr. Merivale.

'I suppose it will be no use my asking to see him?' he said, with a vehement desire in his mind to have just a quarter of an hour's interview with the Major, to tell him exactly what his conduct amounted to. He would have liked to have told him that, if he had told him nothing else.

Perhaps Mary Grove read what was passing in the young man's mind.

'It would be quite no use. It would only make matters worse if you were to see him, and to—to attempt to reason with him. We should only suffer for it. It would make it harder for us to bear.'

Stephen groaned. If he hadn't been recently ordained he might have expressed his feelings more strongly. That uncomfortable dog-collar that was always cutting into his flesh under his chin restrained him. It served as a perpetual reminder.

'Then I'm afraid I cannot help you,' he said, rising.

'No, not in that way; but mother will always be glad to see you. Your visit the other day comforted her so much.'

'Did it, really?' he said, his face brightening; 'I am so glad. I will come again at any time when she can see me. I shall be so glad to be of use to her. May I call to-morrow and see if—if your sister has arrived safely ?'

Mary Grove did not say no, but she smiled—a smile that was a trifle hard—and lifted her lips at the corners.

'You will soon see whether Doll has arrived safely,' she said, her voice almost imperceptibly hardening. 'You will meet her half a dozen times a day in Thorpe. She couldn't be here a day without everybody in Thorpe Regis knowing it.'

CHAPTER IX.

STEPHEN lay awake all night thinking about the inmates of Wellbrook Cottage—to speak more correctly, thinking about Mary Grove and her sister who was coming home so unexpectedly from Germany.

He was not at all sorry that she was coming home. It would be one more in the house—one more woman. He pictured her young and strong, with round, white arms like Nausicaa—three women instead of two against one man, and that a madman.

He wished devoutly that she might already have arrived, that she might be in the house to-night, sleeping under the same roof as those dear women, who were in such hourly peril of their lives.

Suppose the Major should already have murdered them before Doll arrived!

Between sleeping and waking, he drew a picture of Doll, wondering vaguely what her real name might be.

He pictured her tall and strong, large-limbed, and of generous proportions like Mary. She would not be so fair, living abroad—not so white and statue-like; she would have more colour and vivacity. She would bring with her some of the brightness of Continental life. She would be blue-eyed, and have brown hair, with, perhaps, little soft curls on her forehead. He had got as far as the curls when he fell asleep.

When Stephen went his little round the next morning—he usually paid half a dozen parochial visits before dinner, and he taught an hour in the school—he was shocked to find that a man that he ought to have visited the previous day was dead.

He had called in the morning, and the man was asleep, and he had promised to call again in the afternoon ; in the afternoon he had gone to see Mary Grove, and he had forgotten all about it. Now the man was dead ; he was past calling upon—past the reach of preaching and praying.

'An' he was sensible to the last, sir, an' he would have liked to have had a prayer said over him before he died,' said his wife between her sobs, when Stephen called the next day. 'He'd been a wild one in his time, but he was as humble as a little child at the last. "Say a prayer, Mary—say a prayer !" he kep' whisperin', an' I—I was that sick wi' grief that the words stuck in my throat, an' I couldn't say a word !'

Stephen's conscience pricked him dread-

fully all through that day. He had been
neglecting his duty ; he had missed an
opportunity.

He went over to the Rectory in the afternoon, and told his Rector all about it.

He went straight into the study — he
wouldn't see Mrs. Tom — and he passed
Poppy unkindly without a word. He
nodded to her, but he didn't rumple her
hair, or pinch her cheeks, or chase her
across the lawn, or toss her up to the ceiling
of the hall, or exchange any of the customary
amenities with her, and Poppy's feelings were
dreadfully hurt.

The Rector looked grave when Stephen
had told his story. He told it straight-
forwardly, not seeking to exculpate himself
for his forgetfulness. The tears were in his
eyes when he spoke of the man pleading in
vain for one little prayer, and the wife too
choked with grief to utter a word.

'We must leave him to his Master,' the
Rector said gravely—'his Master and ours.
We are quite sure of one thing—that your
neglect will not be visited upon him. Stick
to your duty in future, Dashwood; duty
first, and—and sympathy after. I am sure
we are all very sorry for Miss Grove and
her trials, but there are a great many other
people in the parish to be sorry for.'

'Yes,' said Stephen meekly.

He knew he had earned the rebuke.

'You say the other girl is coming home
to-day unexpectedly? I am very sorry for
that poor woman. I hope this doesn't mean
any fresh trouble for her.'

The Rector discussed the news that
Stephen had told him with his wife at tea,
but he didn't say anything about that
promised visit to poor Will Jones that his
curate had forgotten to pay.

Will Jones was dead—past all praying

for— and there was no use in harrowing
Laura's feelings with the details of that death-
bed repentance.

'Mary Grove's sister is coming back
from Dresden,' he said, ' all of a hurry.'

' What, Doll ?'

'Yes ; Doll, or Dolores, or some such
idiotic name.'

' I think Doll suits her best,' Mrs. Tom
said dryly. 'Doll suits her exactly. What
is she coming home for, and when is she
coming ?'

' She is coming home to-day. Nobody
knows yet what she is coming home for.'

' She has got into a scrape for certain,
and they have sent her away in a hurry. I
shouldn't wonder if they haven't packed her
off at a moment's notice.'

' It would be very unjust if they have.
The people she was with in Dresden were
old friends of Mrs. Grove's, and they would

know how she is situated. It is a cruel thing to send a girl back to such a home.'

' I have no doubt she deserves it !'

' Hush, darling ! don't be too hard upon her. Remember she is down. She is coming back in trouble, perhaps disgrace, and I don't think we should be the first to throw stones at her.'

' I'm afraid I shan't be able to help it,' Mrs. Tom said, shrugging her shoulders. ' I have no patience with Doll—I never had any patience with her little airs and her tricksy ways—and now, when those poor things are in such trouble, to come back upon them is shameful !'

' Perhaps she can't help it. Perhaps she is sent home. Where else could she go but to her home ?'

' I wish she were going anywhere else but here. I am sure we shall have trouble with her. Do you remember how shamefully she

behaved at that tennis-party when we introduced Mr. Dashwood to the parish?'

' I'm afraid I don't remember any special
delinquency of Doll's on that occasion.'

'Oh yes, you must.   She flirted openly
with Mr. Dashwood.   She wouldn't let him
speak to anyone else.   She quite spoiled
the whole thing.   I made up my mind I
would never ask her again.   It was quite
lucky for him that she went to Dresden
the next week; she would have made a
dead set at him.   Nobody knows what
would have happened; and now she is
coming back again !'

' I don't think she will do Dashwood any
harm ; I fancy it's the other one.'

'What, Mary?   Oh, Mary would never
look at him.   She is making a martyr of
herself for the sake of that dreadful man ;
she is not at all the girl to fall in love.   But
Doll, she wouldn't be particular who it was.

I shall call upon Mrs. Grove to-morrow. I dare say she won't see me, but I shall see Mary, and I shall find out all about it. I don't think Doll ought to come back to the parish until there is some explanation—until we know what she has been doing, and what she is sent home for.'

Mrs. Tom had quite decided in her own mind that Doll had 'done something.'

Stephen Dashwood had no heart to call at Wellbrook Cottage to inquire after Mary Grove's sister that day. He had been thinking so much about those dear women, and Doll in particular, that he had neglected his duty.

He didn't fail to tell himself this in pretty round terms. He was rather free in his language when it related to himself. If it hadn't been for Mary Grove's anxiety about her sister he would not have forgotten his promise.

He didn't go near Wellbrook Lane for two whole days, and the amount of visiting he did in that time was prodigious.

He didn't exactly call at every house in the parish, but he looked up all the old women who had ague, and all the old men who were crippled with rheumatism. It was an aguish, rheumaticky place, this sweet green West Country, and all the people who had grown old upon the soil—and there was very little in the cottages except a lime-and-sand floor to separate them from the moist soil beneath—were crippled more or less from rheumatism or shaken with ague. Stephen had his work cut out, and he did it diligently. Once or twice during those penitential days he found his mind wandering in the direction of Wellbrook Lane, when he ought to have been listening to the harrowing details of Betty Broom's ailments.

Betty Broom had a good many for one old woman—she rather prided herself upon their number and variety—and no doubt it relieved her immensely to talk about them. Stephen's mind would wander during the recital—he had heard it before—he wasn't quite sure sometimes, when his wandering attention was recalled suddenly, whether it was the head or the leg that was affected, and his sympathy was sometimes irrelevant.

Old Betty found him out. Poor people have a wonderful knack of finding out whether one's sympathy is real or forced.

They know the genuine thing when they see it. Betty Broom saw that the curate was not listening to her, that he didn't care a button for her aches and pains, and she shut up with a snap, and refused to finish the harrowing tale. It was long enough already, and sad enough, but the curate ought to have listened to it if he couldn't

relieve it. What are curates for but to
listen to sad stories, and to help people to
bear their lot with patience ?

It's of no use preaching to people if you
don't set them an example ; and here was
Stephen, impatient already of even hearing
of the burden the poor old soul had to carry
every day, and yawning in her face, and
mixing up her ailments in a most ridiculous
way.

No wonder Old Betty shut up and refused
to say another word.

Stephen came away dreadfully humiliated ;
the old woman would hardly say good-day
to him. She only turned on her pillow and
groaned. He heard her groaning all the
way down the stairs. He sent in a woman
who lived in an adjoining cottage as he
went by.

' I am afraid Betty Broom is taken worse,'
he said ; ' she is groaning dreadfully.'

'Oh, that's nothing to the way her groans
sometimes!' the woman said cheerfully. 'I
can hear her through the wall, groaning all
night. Her groan'th night an' day when
her's tooked real bad.'

Stephen felt dreadfully ashamed of himself. He couldn't listen for ten consecutive
minutes to the ills that occupied the whole
of the poor old woman's thoughts and attention night and day.

He drew his cap over his eyes—it was
one of those sweet things in felt that can
be dragged into any shape—but it hadn't a
cord and tassel round it. He dragged it
down over his eyes, that were full of penitential tears, and he set his lips hard, and he
walked briskly down the street.

He walked so briskly, and he was so
entirely oblivious of anything that was going
on an inch beyond his nose, that he ran
against a lady coming round the corner.

He turned to beg her pardon, and then he became aware that he was addressing a stranger—a lady he had certainly never seen in Thorpe Regis before.

He had forgotten all about Mary Grove's sister, but he was quite sure, from the brief glance he got of the stranger as he turned the corner, and nearly knocked her down, that it was Doll.

She was not the least like Mary.

She was *petite* and fair, and had an immense nimbus of fluffy, golden-brown hair, and she had the most glorious eyes in the world—at least, they looked so to Stephen in that brief glance he had of them.

She really wasn't unlike a doll. Pink and white, red-lipped, round-eyed, and with beautiful fluffy hair.

The sight of her after Betty Broom and her groanings seemed almost a mockery.

Let us hope that Betty will not always

groan; that she, too, will be young and fair some day—fairer than the daughters of men.

Stephen was quite right in his conclusions; it really was Doll.

She was in the garden when he called at Wellbrook Cottage the next day; he couldn't put off calling any longer.

His penance was over; he had paid all those visits; he had done various works of supererogation; the balance of duty was on the right side; and he called at Wellbrook Cottage with a quiet mind. His mind was so free and unembarrassed, indeed — perhaps it was the reaction of those penitential tears—that he ran up the steps of the cottage—he took them two at a time — instead of climbing them slowly and soberly, as befitted a curate making a parochial visit.

It was not exactly a parochial visit. It

was like the fairy prince going up the steps of the sleeping palace. His heart was beating with expectation ; he did not know what he should find.

After that vision of yesterday, he thought he should light on something fair.

He was not disappointed.

The small servant-maid opened the door to him. She was smarter than usual, and had a bow of ribbon in her cap. He didn't know why he remarked this detail, but he remembered it afterwards when he recalled this day. She wore a smile as well as a bow, and he thought—he might have been mistaken—that there was a twinkle in her eyes when he asked if the ladies were at home.

Oh, if Mary Grove had seen that twinkle !

She showed him into the little room where the books were, and the familiar photographs, and the water-colour sketch of Girton.

The glass door that led out into the garden was open, and Mary was coming to him across the grass. It was but a little strip of grass, with boughs of trees over-hanging it—the boughs, he remembered, on which the lines were strung and the clothes were hanging on the day of his first visit.

There were no clothes hanging there now, but there was a hammock swung between the branches in the coolest, shadiest spot. The lawn was not smooth or well-kept, but it was green—delightfully green—which is more than well-kept lawns in scorching August days often are. It was choked with dandelions, and tall yellow-eyed daisies, and clover in bloom, and scarlet pimpernel, and it had no edges to speak of; it didn't leave off anywhere in particular.

It was no good for tennis or croquet; it

was only fit to sit on in the sweet, dusky
shade of the apple-laden branches overhead,
or to hang up clothes in. It would be a
lovely place for drying clothes on a windy
March day, when the apple-trees were bare,
and the playful east wind frolicked among
the wet garments, and filled them out as
their owners were not accustomed to fill
them.

There were no clothes hanging there to-
day; no corpulent bodies or gouty limbs
swinging spasmodically on the line. There
was only a low chair, and a work-table, and
a hammock swinging in a cool corner.

The little green garden was certainly
sweeter without the wet clothes. The
flower-borders were visible, and a rustic
bower covered with honeysuckle. There
was nothing in the flower-borders to speak
of—only yellow marigolds and mignonette,
a bush of lavender, and some sweet, old-

fashioned lad's-love ; and there were monthly roses and sweet-smelling white jasmine climbing over the garden wall.

It was all sweet-smelling and homely, and seemed as if it had grown up of itself—as if a gardener had never set foot in the little green enclosure since it was first planted.

' Doll is in the garden,' Mary Grove said, when the formal greeting was over. ' She has put up a hammock, and has swung herself to sleep.'

' And your mother ?' he said hurriedly.

He was glad to ask about Mrs. Grove, to give himself time. His heart was beating so ridiculously that he couldn't trust himself to speak about Doll.

' Oh, mother is so much better for Doll's coming—better and brighter! She looks years younger in these few days ; she is looking almost like her old self. She is so wrapped up in Doll.'

'And your father?' he ventured to say.

'Oh, papa is changed too. Doll's coming has done him a world of good. He has been better, so much better, since she came back. He has not disturbed us at all of nights. I hope the change will last. It has been quite wonderful. I think that is why we are all feeling so much brighter and better.'

She was certainly looking brighter, and there was some colour in her cheeks, and a light in her eyes. Her eyes were as steady and as serious as ever, but they were softer. A woman's eyes ought to be soft, and Mary Grove's were rather hard. Perhaps her lot had been hard lately, but they were softening now. If Doll had done nothing else, she had taken the edge—just the edge only —off Nausicaa's hard lot, and had cleared her brow.

'Do you think now, now that your sister

is here, before the freshness of her coming
wears away, that it would be a good time
for me to see Major Grove? He might
listen to me now, when he would refuse,
perhaps altogether, to see me by-and-by.'

Stephen asked the question eagerly. He
was quite honest and sincere in his desire
to reach Mary Grove's father, but, with the
words on his lips, his heart was out in the
green garden, in that cool spot under the
apple-trees where Doll was swinging in her
hammock.

He had come there to see—well, he didn't
know what he had come to see, but, with
that magic music beating in his heart, he
hadn't come so joyfully up the steps of
Wellbrook Cottage to see a raving madman.

CHAPTER X.

DOLL.

'More close and close his footsteps wind ;
The magic music in his heart
Beats quick and quicker, till he find
The quiet chamber far apart.'

'We must ask Doll,' Mary Grove said, as she walked across the grass by his side. 'She has so much influence over papa ; she can do anything with him.'

They were approaching the hammock swung between the branches of the apple-trees, and Stephen's heart was beating faster and faster.

He was feeling more and more like the fairy prince. He didn't at all know what he was going to find. The hammock covered up every inch of Doll except a bit of ribbon, which was fluttering idly in the breeze.

It was a bit of pink ribbon, and it looked like the end of a sash.

He saw the ribbon, and he flushed up with quite a guilty feeling. He almost felt as if he were treading on sacred ground. He didn't dare approach the hammock ; he stood blushing ridiculously a couple of yards off while Mary Grove called to her sister.

'Doll ! Doll !'

There came no response from the hammock, and Mary Grove called again.

'Doll ! Doll ! It's no use your pretending to be asleep ; you are no more asleep than I am !' she said sharply ; and she gave the hammock a shake that ought to have aroused any moderate sleeper, but it didn't awake Doll.

She refused to be awakened by any sisterly admonition ; clearly it was time for the fairy prince to step in.

Stephen had approached a yard nearer— he couldn't help it—and he could see quite clearly into the hammock.

He saw—well, it doesn't matter what he really saw ; it depends so much on one's eyes and heart and brain what one does see. We colour everything with our own fancies and emotions ; we create the atmosphere, and the atmosphere gives the tone to the picture.

Stephen, with his spirit fluttering like a lark, and that poppy colour in his cheeks, saw a vision he never forgot. It was only a girl in a summer frock curled up in a hammock, and wilfully keeping her eyes close shut. To Stephen it was a goddess on a summer cloud—a red-lipped goddess, golden-haired, amid billows of soft white muslin draperies. A pink and white goddess, too, with dark, level brows and dark lashes — long lashes that lay like a fringe upon her cheeks, and made him wonder what colour the eyes might be beneath.

Women would have likened the sleeping figure to a doll in a cradle—a lovely wax doll — delicately tinted and beautifully arranged ; they wouldn't have compared it to a woman — a real woman — live with sorrow and sin, live with pain and with passion.

Stephen compared her to a goddess. Should he go on his knee and awake her like the fairy prince of old?

' Nonsense, Doll ; wake up!' Mary said sharply, shaking the hammock vigorously, and nearly shaking the sleeper out.

Doll yawned, and showed her teeth. They were lovely little white teeth, and they were worth showing. She didn't open her mouth wide, like some people do in yawning, and show a dreadful gaping red cavern. She yawned very nicely, and disclosed two rows of very white teeth. She opened her eyes by degrees—not all at once—taking just a peep at the blue sky, and the waving green boughs overhead, through her dark lashes.

She never looked in the direction of Stephen. How should she know that the fairy prince had been watching her for the last five minutes, and was ready at any moment to do all that the situation required of him?

Ready and waiting.

' Get up, Doll! Mr. Dashwood has called to see you.'

The speaker's voice was impatient, not to say scornful, and Stephen remarked, with as much surprise as he was just then capable

of feeling, that it was very unlike Mary
Grove's usual voice. It wasn't a bit soft,
or tender, or sisterly.

Doll opened her eyes in surprise, as if the
curate's visit were the most unexpected thing
in the world, as if she hadn't spent an hour
before her glass that afternoon arranging
herself for it. She blushed like a red, red
rose when she saw a man on the grass, and
she sprang out of the hammock and stood
before him, rosy and downcast, amid the
billows of white muslin.

It was exactly like Venus rising from the
sea.

At least, Stephen made that idiotic comparison.

'Oh, Mary-gold, why didn't you wake
me!' she said reproachfully.

Mary Grove didn't exactly sniff, but she
smiled that hard little smile of hers that
lifted the corners of her lips.

'I did everything short of turning you out upon the grass,' she said sweetly ; and then she introduced her sister Dolores to Mr. Banister's curate.

He had divined rightly when he met Doll outside Betty Broom's cottage—the girl he had run against was Mary Grove's sister-- and then all at once he recognised her as the girl he had met at that tennis-party at the Rectory a year ago. He hadn't taken very much notice of her then ; he had time to observe her more closely now. He could see exactly what she was like. He could see that her hair wasn't pale, or flaxen, or golden, like other women's ; it was the colour the Old Masters loved to paint. It was the colour of Raphael's Madonnas, and Titian's Magdalenes, and Rubens' women—a warm, rich auburn that sunbeams lost themselves among.

Her eyes ought to have been blue, but

they matched her hair, and were changing in their hue—hazel sometimes, and shining like wine sparkling in the cup.

She was utterly unlike Mary—as unlike as two sisters could be. Mary Grove was bounteously made, like a goddess; but Dolores was *petite*—a slender, childish little figure, with sweet wine-coloured eyes that were inexpressibly wistful beneath their shining.

Stephen thought her the loveliest creature he had ever seen in his life, and the words stuck in his throat when he tried to speak to her. She was quite as engaging as she was sweet, and she thanked him in the prettiest manner for the kindness he had shown her mother, and Mary-gold—she always spoke of her sister as Mary-gold—and the interest he had taken in her ' poor father.'

At the mention of her father her eyes brimmed over.

They were such sweet downcast eyes, and they brimmed over so readily.

Stephen wasn't aware that he had shown any kindness in particular to Mrs. Grove and her daughter, or any interest in her reprobate old father to call for tears ; but he was touched—distinctly touched.

' I shall be so glad to be of use !' he murmured ; 'your sister thinks that with your help I may be able to reach him. If you could make the opportunity, I would come to him at any time. I am sure we must not lose a chance.'

Dolores looked at him through her tears ; her eyes were not so blurred that she did not see that he was a tall young man, rather slight in figure, that he had straight, regular features, and that he was clean-shaven, and had a sensitive mouth, and his eyes were earnest and grave in expression.

' Oh no !' she said eagerly ; ' we must not

lose a chance. You really think there is
—a—a chance—of—of poor papa's re-
covery ?'

' I hope so,' he said earnestly.

'Oh, Mr. Dashwood, if you only knew
what it meant to us! We have lost everything through this terrible thing that has
happened to poor papa. We have lost our
home, our position, our friends—all—everything! Oh, it is dreadful! We, who were
brought up so differently, reduced to this
—this dreadful place! Cut off from everybody—from everything ; nobody will notice
us now, and nobody calls ; and—and we
have to work for our living !'

Dolores' voice rose to a wail as she ended
this dismal summary, but Mary Grove
looked on unmoved, only her eyes
hardened.

' I don't think that is the hardest part,'
she said gravely ; ' it is the dreadful wreck

that poor papa has become, and the trial it
is to mother—poor mother !'

It was always her cry—' poor mother !'

' Ah! you don't feel things so keenly,
Mary-gold, you are so wrapped up in your
work.   You Girton girls don't see things
like other people.   You are above society
and that sort of thing.   You don't realize
what it is to poor little me—to be cut off
from everything ; to have no tennis-parties,
no dances, no new gowns, and to grind all
one's days in a horrible stuffy schoolroom.
Oh, it's cruel—it's horrible !'

The poor little thing subsided into tears,
and Mary Grove looked coolly on.

' I don't think weeping about it will mend
it,' she said, in a most unsympathetic voice.
' Mr. Dashwood knows exactly what it is.
Mother has told him all about it—all ; she
has kept nothing back.   He knows the
terror that we live in by night and by day,

and that everybody is afraid to come near us. Papa has frightened everybody away.'

' Not everybody,' Stephen said, looking for the first time at the elder sister. He was moved to see how steady her eyes were, and her face was calm and grave. She was quite reconciled to her lot ; she had grown used to it. The spectacle of her own loss and trial and sacrifice didn't move her in the least. ' I don't think Major Grove will frighten me away. I have only been waiting for an opportunity. Now that you have come, I hope you will make the opportunity.'

Stephen was tremendously in earnest. He didn't exactly know what he was going to say or do to Major Grove ; whether he was going to exorcise the evil spirit by any of the ancient modes of healing, or whether, coming down to more prosaic modern forms,

he was going to prevail upon him to sign
the pledge and join the Blue Ribbon Army.

He hadn't made up his mind what he was
going to do.   He was waiting for an opportunity to do something, and Dolores promised him, before he went away, that she
would make that opportunity.

'If I get papa, in the humour to see you,
will you come at any time I send for you?'
she said.   'It may be late at night ; it may
be early in the morning.   Will you come at
once, whenever I send?'

'I will come at once,' he said.

Mrs. Grove did not appear during his
visit.   She was sitting with her husband ;
she could not leave him a minute.

'Oh, Mary-gold!' Doll exclaimed in her
exaggerated little way when he had gone, and
throwing herself into the low chair beside
the work-table, 'we have found a champion !
We have found someone to fight our battles.

It is like a story of the Middle Ages. We are two distressed damsels shut up in a castle with a dragon—a cruel, wicked dragon —and he is going to slay the dragon and rescue us. He will have to marry one of us ; we can't say no, Mary-gold, if he really rescues us. I wonder which of us he is going to marry.'

'You need not wonder. If he married anybody, he would marry you.'

'Me? Oh no; he wouldn't marry me poor little me! He would marry you, Mary-gold. He would choose the best— men always choose the best. You would keep him a knight-errant always ; you would fill him with noble ambitions ; while I—I should drag him down off his pedestal. A champion wouldn't marry me.'

Dolores' face was flushed, and her eyes were soft, and her heart was beating fast under her white bodice, as she spoke of the knight - errant who was coming to marry Mary-gold.

'I don't think Mr. Dashwood is coming here to marry anybody,' Mary said severely. 'He is very good to take an interest in us ; everybody else has given us up—everybody but Mrs. Banister ; she had not called for months until she called yesterday——'

'She only called to find out why I had come back,' interrupted Doll, with a sudden scarlet colour coming into her cheeks. 'She thought I had done *something*, and she wanted to find out what it was. Oh, you needn't thank her for calling, Mary-gold ; I know exactly why she called.'

'I'm afraid she went away disappointed, then, though I don't see any reason why she shouldn't have been told. She would have seen that you could have done nothing else but come home. You couldn't have stayed in the place a single day after——'

'No,' Doll interrupted hurriedly, with that scarlet colour glowing in her cheeks, 'of course I couldn't! But I don't think we need talk about it, Mary-gold; we are not bound to explain to people why I came back in a hurry. We are not bound to tell people that that man—that horrid, horrid man—made it impossible for me to stay a day longer. People here would put a different colour on the story. There is no knowing what they would say!'

'No—o; there is no knowing. But Mrs. Banister would say you had done right to come home. I think we must tell her, Doll; I should like her to know the truth. She will think there is some mystery in it, and I hate mysteries.'

'She would be sure to think that I was to blame, that—that I had given the man some encouragement. She wouldn't understand the hot, passionate nature of foreigners.

She would think everybody was cold and
dull and proper like her husband. She has
never seen a man infatuated — madly infatuated — a man who loves the air you
breathe, who would go down upon his knees
to kiss the print of your footsteps on the
ground.'

'No; I should hope not! I am sure
Mr. Banister never went down on his knees
to kiss the ground his wife had trod upon,
and a man has no right to kiss anybody
else's footsteps.'

'No—o, perhaps not ; but they do.'

And Doll laughed a little low laugh, as if
the recollection of the horrid, horrid man
who used to kiss her footprints were not so
very hateful, although she had run away
from him, or been sent away, which was
much the same thing ; it was only another
way of putting it.

CHAPTER XI.

MAJOR GROVE.

THE opportunity that Doll had promised to make came earlier than Stephen Dashwood expected. It came the next day.

He had just sat down to his frugal mid-day meal, which represented both lunch and dinner, when a note was put into his hands. It was a hastily-scribbled note, and it was written in pencil ; it was from Doll.

It was dreadfully badly written ; it was scrawled all over the page in a sprawling, untidy hand ; it was not in the least like Mary Grove's beautiful neat writing.

'Papa will see you,' the letter ran, 'if you

will come *at once*.   A terrible thing has happened to mamma — a seizure of some kind—and the doctor does not think she will recover.   Papa is broken down ;   he thinks he has killed her.   If you come *now* he may listen to you.

'Yours in haste,

'Doll.'

Stephen didn't stay to eat his dinner.   He left the mutton - chop that did duty for that double meal untasted, and hurried away.

He was so afraid of being late that he ran nearly all the way to Wellbrook Cottage.

He met the Baroness Eberlein and Bébée driving just outside the town, and the Baroness stopped the pony-chaise when he came up to her, and called to him to stop ; but he only nodded to her, and ran on.

'Where can he be going at that pace?'

she said to Bébée impatiently. 'I think he might have stopped a minute. I was going to ask him to come in to supper. He hasn't been in to supper for a long time.'

'P'raps somebody's ill,' Bébée suggested. 'I shouldn't wonder if that dreadful Major Grove hasn't killed somebody. Mr. Dashwood was afraid he would kill those poor women.'

'Bother the poor women!' muttered the Baroness sulkily; 'he might have stopped to speak to me!'

And then she gave the unoffending old pony a sharp cut across his ears, and drove back to the town. She always took it out of the first dumb creature she came across if anything happened to go wrong with her. It was one of her gracious foreign ways.

Stephen arrived breathless at Wellbrook Cottage. He had time to cool himself and recover his breath while he waited on the steps. He had to ring twice before the door was opened. It was opened at last by the small servant - maid. Her eyes were red, as if she had been crying, and her face had a tired, soddened look, as if she had been up all night, and she had on a dreadfully dirty apron, and her cap was awry.

She opened the door a few inches, and put out her untidy head and her dirty cap.

'Oh!' she said, with an air of relief, 'it's you. I thought it was the perlice.'

'Why did you think it was the police?' Stephen asked, when he had got both his feet on the mat. He never felt sure in that house until he was well on the mat; he always expected the door to be shut in his face.

'Oh, because there's been such a rumpus! He was orful last night'—she pointed with her thumb as she spoke in the direction of the room that Major Grove occupied. 'He tried to kill all three of 'em ; an' the missus, her fell down in a fit, an' he thought he'd a-killed her, an' that sobered him all of a suddent. He's been a-cryin' like a babby all the morning, an' he keeps sayin' the perlice are after him. He wouldn't let me open the door when you ringed first ; he said it were the perlice.'

'Leah, Leah !' a voice called impatiently from the end of the passage. The glass-door that led into the garden was closed, the shutter had not been taken down, and the passage was in darkness ; but Stephen recognised the voice.

It was the voice of Doll.

'Who are you talking to, Leah ? If it is the doctor, take him upstairs at once.'

'It is not the doctor,' said Stephen, stepping forward ; 'it is I. I happened to

be at home when your letter arrived, and I
came away at once.'

'So soon?' she said; 'we did not expect
you so soon. The messenger we sent with
the letter has not come back yet. It is
very good of you to come at once. Oh,
you don't know what trouble we are in!'

He took both the hands that she had
stretched out to him, and he led her into
the little room at the end of the passage,
the door of which was open—Mary-gold's
room. The blinds were still drawn down,
as if it were night, and the windows were
closed, and the air of the room was close
and stuffy. Nobody seemed to have remembered to draw up the blinds or open the
shutters.

'I am so sorry——' Stephen began, and
stopped.

He was so shocked by the change in Doll
that he couldn't go on; he was obliged to stop.

The Doll of to-day was not the Doll of yesterday.

All the pretty colour had gone out of her cheeks—the pretty brilliant colour that made her eyes so bright, and contrasted with the pearly white of her skin.

It was quite gone now, as if it had been washed out, and her eyes were swollen with weeping, and looked washed out, too, and her beautiful hair was gathered up in an untidy little knot. Stephen remarked that all the curl had gone out of it, too, and that her nose was red—decidedly red. One cannot weep all night without getting a red nose, and it was dreadfully mean of Stephen at such a time to make comparisons.

Perhaps if he had not come quite so soon, if he had been as tardy as the messenger who had not yet come back, Doll would have been better prepared to receive him. She would have had time to bathe her eyes,

and smooth her hair, and look in the glass,
and—and he would not have had occasion to
make that odious comparison.

He should have lingered over his mutton-
chop, and walked quietly through the town,
and chatted by the way with the Baroness,
instead of tearing through the streets in that
mad fashion.

'We've had a dreadful night!' Doll said,
speaking hurriedly, and turning her back to
the light that he should not see her
miserable face. 'Papa has nearly murdered
us all. He was so violent after you had
gone; he thought we had let someone in
the house—a keeper, who had come to take
him away. He would not be persuaded to
go to bed; he sat up all night watching, for
the man, he thought, was hiding somewhere,
and he had armed himself with a poker : we
could not take it away. He seemed to doze
off about daybreak, and mamma made us,

Mary-gold and me, lie down. We had not been out of the room five minutes before we heard a scream and a fall, and—and when we opened the door mamma was on the floor insensible, and papa was standing over her with the poker.'

'Good heavens!' said Stephen, turning as white as the girl before him ; 'had—had he struck her ?'

'We don't know ; we fear he had. She has not been conscious since.'

'How did you get the poker from him ?'

'Mary-gold took it from him. I couldn't go near him, I was so dreadfully afraid. He was brandishing it over his head like a mad-man ; he would have killed anyone who had gone near him.'

'How did Mary-gold—how did your sister take it from him ?'

'Oh, Mary-gold is not frightened of him like I am. She lifted mamma up, and told him he had murdered her. She thought he had. " Look, look," she said, " at your wicked work ! She is dead, quite dead !" The sight of mamma on the floor and Mary-gold's words seemed to sober him for a moment, and he let his arm that was brandishing the poker fall, and she took it from him.'

' And your mother ?'

' Oh, mamma has not spoken since. We carried her to bed and sent for a doctor : he thinks it is a seizure ; he cannot tell whether he has really struck her ; but papa believes that he has murdered her ; his remorse is dreadful !'

' I should think so !' said Stephen indignantly.

' He has been weeping all the morning, ever since the doctor told him mamma was not likely to recover. He is quite sober now, and we thought if he is ever to be reached it would be now, while he is full of remorse for what he has done.'

'Surely,' said Stephen, but he said it with a shiver of repugnance. He had no heart for the task he had undertaken. He could hardly trust himself to speak to the miserable bully and coward who had led these dear women such a terrible life, and had ended by murdering one of them.

'I think you must go and see mamma first,' Doll said, in a flat, hopeless voice, and with her eyes brimming over; 'you must make your visit to mamma a reason for coming. She will not know you; she doesn't know anybody.'

Stephen followed her upstairs into the room where Mrs. Grove lay. The blinds were down in this room, like they were in the rest of the house. Mary Grove was sitting beside the bed, and she was applying some cooling lotion to the poor woman's

head. She looked up when Stephen entered,
but she did not take any notice of him ; she
still continued applying the lotion. In that
dim light Stephen could see that her face
was as white as the face on the pillow, white
and set; only the face on the pillow was
calm and placid, all the lines were smoothed
out of it, while the girl's face was white and
drawn ; it looked ten years older than when
he had seen it yesterday.

'How is she?' he asked softly, as he
stood bareheaded beside the bed.

'She will never be any better,' said the
girl in a hard voice that with an effort she
kept from breaking. 'It is a seizure—and—
and she is not likely to recover.'

'You think it is a seizure?' Stephen said
softly, but his eyes asked a different question.

'Hush! Of course it is a seizure!'

She looked across the bed at Doll as she
spoke, and Doll dropped her eyes.

' I couldn't help it, Mary-gold! I couldn't
indeed !' she sobbed. ' I was obliged to tell
Mr. Dashwood the truth. How could he
speak to papa if he didn't know the truth ?'

'We do not know ourselves yet, Doll.
We are not at all sure that—that it is not
a seizure ; so many people mamma's age are
suddenly cut off like this, and mamma has
been tried a good deal lately, and she has
not been so strong as usual——'

' She was quite well when we left her,
five minutes before we heard her scream and
fall, Mary, and papa was standing over her
when we came back with——'

' Hush !' Mary Grove said sternly ; ' hush !
would you betray your own father, Doll ?
No one saw it but ourselves—and—and we
must give him the benefit of the doubt.'

'Of course you must give him the benefit
of the doubt,' Stephen murmured ; he could
not but see how that cruel night's work had

shaken Mary Grove, and how desperately
she was trying to shield her father.

'You will go and see papa,' she said, but
she did not look at Stephen, she was so
occupied applying the lotion ; 'and you will
make him understand—that—that this would
not have happened but for the continual
strain that mamma has had for so long, and
that she has broken down under it. He is
overwhelmed with grief, and now, while he
is softened and penitent, he may listen to
you.'

Stephen bowed his head in silence and
followed Doll out of the room.

'I couldn't help it,' Doll sobbed, when
she had got outside. 'I was obliged to tell
you the truth. If mamma dies, he has
killed her. Oh, I don't know how I shall
ever look at him again!'

What comfort could Stephen give her?

'She may not die,' he said softly, but he

could not say it hopefully; ' she ·may recover. You must pray for her—and for him.'

' Oh, I can't pray for him ; I can't forgive him! I can't bear to speak to him ; his tears and his grief do not affect me like they do Mary-gold She thinks of nothing but sheltering him. She will never forgive me for having told you.'

' Your secret is safe with me,' Stephen said gravely.

And then he followed the weeping girl down the stairs.

In that sad house, in the face of such tragedies, he had ceased to remark the change in Doll. He thought her sister was hard upon her—decidedly hard upon her.

Major Grove was sitting in the arm-chair before the fire. It was the middle of August, but there was a fire burning in the grate, and the Major was cowering over it with his face buried in his hands.

A sad, drooping figure, with bowed head and shrunken shoulders—the figure of a man who had been beaten in the battle of life, and had thrown up the game.

The attitude of the man as he cowered over the embers in the grate was inexpressibly sad. He had heard the door open, and the strange footstep on the floor, and he raised his head slowly, with a hopeless ashen misery in his face that went to Stephen's heart, in spite of all his prejudice.

'So you have come for me?' he said sadly, speaking in a low thrilling voice, with something in it that reminded Stephen of Mary Grove. 'I am quite ready. I have been expecting you all day. She is dead, and—and I have killed her!'

'No; she is not dead, and you have not

killed her,' said Stephen reassuringly. ' Please God she will not die.'

' Oh yes, she will die. He told me to kill her. He has told me so often to kill her, and I had not the heart to. She has been a good wife to me—a good mother to her children ; there was never a better wife or a better mother, and—I have killed her !'

He let his face fall into his hands again, and he shivered and cowered over the fire. Stephen could see his thin shoulders quivering beneath his shabby coat, which hung so loosely upon him, and his lean white hands trembling as they supported his drooping head.

It was a miserable picture.

It disarmed Stephen's anger, and it brought the tears to his eyes.

To think that a man could fall so low !

' Are you going to take me away ?' he

asked presently, in his sad, hopeless voice. The voice was like the face he raised to Stephen's as he spoke—unutterably hopeless and sad.

'No,' Stephen said, speaking as re-assuringly as he could; 'I am not come to take you away. Why should I? You are not responsible to man for what you have done. You are only responsible to God.'

'Stop!' said the Major hastily, with a sudden light coming in his dull eyes—'stop! I am responsible to Him no longer. He has given me up. He has sent—that—that Other—to—to torment me before the time. I am not my own master. I am responsible —to—to no one but to him!'

He spoke rapidly, in disconnected sentences, and there was a strange wildness in his eyes that Stephen had never seen in any eyes before.

'Oh yes, you are!' he said, sitting down on a chair on the opposite side of the fire-place, and speaking in an easy, assured manner, as if this were an afternoon call and the subject an everyday topic. 'You are as responsible as I am to your own Master—each to his own. There is only one Master for us, you know; we cannot serve another. The enemy may take us prisoner, but he can't make us serve him against our will. We have all of us free will, thank God!'

The Major shook his head.

'You don't know,' he said—'oh, you don't know!'

And then Stephen looked up, and saw Doll standing by the door watching them. Her eyes were dilated, and her pretty brows were knit, and her mouth was drawn and hard. She was looking at the pitiful sight with unutterable disgust and loathing.

There was not a gleam of compassion in her beautiful eyes. The pity of it did not move her one whit.

' I think you had better leave us alone for the present,' Stephen said, when he saw her standing there.

And he got up and held the door open for her to pass out, and closed it after her.

CHAPTER XII.

A MIRACLE.

THE Rector of Thorpe Regis was sitting in his study after lunch on that same afternoon —it was a Saturday afternoon—preparing his sermon for the following day.

He usually left the preparation of his Sunday sermons until the Saturday; it was not a commendable practice, but, as he explained, they had the benefit of simmering in his mind all the week, and were not the raw, undigested things they would have been if he had sat down and written them off-hand on Monday morning.

The simmering process that had been

going on all the week had not produced any great results. It had only produced two texts, and he was still undecided which text he should settle upon, when from his study-window he saw his curate, Stephen Dash-wood, tearing across the lawn.

He ought to have been too much engrossed with his rival texts to have looked out of window, but Tom Banister was very fond of looking out of window.

It was a convenient window to look out of; he had only to raise his eyes from his work, and there was the window just in front of them. It ought to have looked out upon a back wall, or a laurel hedge, or a kitchen-garden; it ought not to have presented any temptation to the scholar and student within to take his eyes from his book, or his manu-script, if it had any claim to be called ' a study window.'

Instead of this the study window of the

Rectory looked out on a broad sunny lawn. The lawn was all ablaze now with brilliant beds of scarlet geraniums and blue lobelias ; it was trim and close-shaven, and there were noble trees upon it that cast cool, delightful shadows on the smooth grass ; and there were two children playing on the lawn.

It was the ordinary thing. A green expanse, not very big, but soft and mossy and well mown, shaded by some fine old beeches, and a thick hedge of evergreens shutting out the road beyond. There was nothing remarkable in it, only green grass and a blaze of scarlet blossoms, and the pleasant shade of some old trees.

There are hundreds of rectory houses with exactly the same things, but to Tom Banister, looking out of his study window, when he ought to have been looking at the manuscript page before him, on which to-

morrow's sermon was to be written, it was
the fairest picture in the world.

There was something quite remarkable
about those old beeches—there always is
about one's own trees ; there was never a
better-kept lawn ; the colour of that blue
lobelia border was a shade deeper than any
other lobelia border in the county. It was
as blue as heaven itself.

Heaven and home were not very far
separated in Tom Banister's mind. The
terms were nearly synonymous.

He couldn't keep his wandering attention
from straying from his sermon to the green
pleasance outside on this bright afternoon.
Poppy and Tommykin were out there, playing on the lawn, and every time their happy
laughter was wafted in at the open study
window he looked up.

He was looking up when he saw his
curate dashing in that unaccustomed way,

with his long coat-tails flying behind him, across the grass.

'Not now, Tommykin ; not now, Poppy,' Stephen said breathlessly, as the children tried to stop him in his flight.

He distanced them, and reached the hall door, which stood open, before them.

Poppy pouted and turned back, but Tommykin, with his finger in his mouth, stood looking after the curate.

'Somefing's going to happen; I fink,' he remarked, with an air of immense wisdom. 'Let's do and see!'

So they went to see. That is, they ran over to the open study window, and stood on tip-toe looking in.

Two bright faces, two pairs of shining eyes, and, oh ! such a confusion of little curly wigs.

'I —I have come for the pledge-book,' Dashwood said, or, rather, panted, as he

burst into the Rector's study ; ' Major Grove
is going to sign the pledge !'

' Major Grove ?'

' Yes ; Major Grove. He has——' He
was going to say, ' He has nearly killed his
wife, and now, in a fit of remorse, he is
ready to do anything,' but he remembered
himself in time. ' He is willing and anxious
to sign the pledge.'

' He'll never keep it if he signs it. It'll
only be a farce.'

' Let him try it. For Heaven's sake let
him try it ! Give him a chance. He is in
earnest now, at any rate ; he swears he will
never taste the accursed thing again !'

The Rector shrugged his shoulders. He
had not much faith in Major Grove. He
had lived longer than Dashwood, and he
knew more about human nature. He knew,
or he thought he knew, exactly how weak it
was. He had seen so many pledges broken.

He went over to a shelf and took down a book, the book wherein the temperance pledges of the neighbourhood were written.

There were hundreds of pledges in that shabby book, and nearly all of them had been broken. Some had been renewed time after time, and few, very few, had been faithfully kept.

It was like the pavement of the nether regions; it was a miserable record of good intentions.

'I wish you success,' the Rector said, as he put the book in Dashwood's hands. 'If you can persuade him to keep the pledge after he has signed it, you will have done more than I have been able to do. You will have worked a miracle. How long has he been in this mind?'

'Only now. I have just left him. I hurried here to get the book as quick as possible, in case——'

' In case he should change his mind,' said the Rector. ' Exactly. I'm afraid if your protégé can't be trusted half an hour without risk of his changing his mind, there will be small chance of his keeping the pledge after he has signed it.'

' No,' Stephen said sadly ; ' no, perhaps not ; still, we must give him the chance. His intention is good, and he is in earnest, if ever a man was in earnest ; and, after all, if he fall, if he have not strength to stand— we are all weak, God knows, miserably weak ! —he is answerable to his own Master.'

' Yes,' said Banister gravely. ' He is the judge, not we. To his own Master he stands or falls ; He only knows the strength of the temptation, and—and the weakness of His poor tried servant. Take the book, Dashwood, and God give the poor wretch strength to keep the pledge when he has taken it !'

Poppy, with her elbows on the window-sill and her chin in her hands, and Tommy-kin on his 'tippety-toe,' as Poppy termed it, were spectators of the interview, and watched Stephen crossing the lawn with the pledge-book under his arm.

' I said we was doing to see somefing,' Tommykin said, in his oracular manner, removing a damp forefinger from his mouth to give effect to the utterance. ' Dare is doing to be a miracle '—only he called it ' miwacle.'

Banister's sermons had to simmer in his mind for the rest of the afternoon. He couldn't apply himself to settling the rival claims of the texts that were balancing themselves in his mind after that interview. He had to call Mrs. Tom down, and talk Stephen's errand over with her.

' What's he been doing ?' she asked, when Tom told her his news. ' I'm sure Major Grove wouldn't do anything of the kind if

he weren't driven up in a corner. I shouldn't
wonder if he hasn't nearly murdered some
of those women, and he's frightened out of
his wits, or into his wits.'

Mrs. Tom was not far wrong.

The doctor was at Wellbrook Cottage
when Stephen got back. He had just come
down from seeing Mrs. Grove, and he had
told the weeping girls that their mother
might not live through the night.

' I am very glad you have come,' he said
to Stephen. ' I wanted to talk to you about
that madman. He is not fit to be left alone
with only women in the house. He may
break out again at any moment and murder
them all.'

Then Stephen told him about his talk
with Major Grove, his grief and repentance,
and his desire to sign the pledge.

The doctor, who knew Major Grove of
old, smiled when he heard about the pledge.

'Try him,' he said, 'try him by all means.
He will break it in twenty-four hours.'

Nobody had any faith in him, not even
his own children. Mary Grove shook her
head, and Doll laughed outright, when
Stephen produced his book.

The Major was in his old place by the
fire, sitting in his old attitude, with his
face in his hands and his elbows resting
on his knees, when Stephen went into his
room with the book. The fire had gone
nearly out, but he still crouched over the
few dying embers in the nearly empty
grate.

'I have brought the book,' Stephen said
cheerfully when he had closed the door.

The Major looked up. His face was
pale, almost bloodless, and his eyes were
wild and bloodshot. His hands were trembling, and his lips quivering, and his voice
shook like his hands.

'It will be no use,' he said in a hollow, hopeless voice ; 'it will be no use my signing anything. I am ready, quite ready, God knows, to sign anything, to promise anything, if it will be any good ; but it will not be—it will be only a form, a mockery ! I warn you it will be no good. It will only be holding out a rope of sand to a drowning man. I shall break it the moment the temptation comes to me. I shall not be able to keep it a day—an hour.'

'Oh yes, you will be able to keep it,' Stephen said reassuringly ; and then he opened his book at a fair unsullied page, and laid a nice clean piece of blotting paper across it, and dipped a new pen in the ink. He had got the new pen and the blotting paper from Mary Grove's room, while Doll looked on in scornful silence. She had no faith in her drunken old father ; she had no patience with him.

'You will not take the promise in your
own strength, you know, and if you are
kept, you will be kept by the power of God.
He will with the temptation give you a way
of escape.'

The Major shook his head.

' Oh, you don't know !' he said, or moaned.
'You don't know! How should you? You
have never felt what it is. I tell you, if I
were holden with cords of steel, when this
thirst comes upon me I should burst them.
I have struggled—God only knows how I
have struggled against it! You don't think,
young man, that I have made no resistance
—that I have given in without a struggle ?'

There was a dignity about the wretched
man as he spoke that touched Stephen ;
some latent fire of his lost manliness lingered, and a dull-red glow crept up under
his skin.

' No,' said Stephen warmly ; ' I am sure

you have made a resistance ; if not for your own sake, for the sake of your wife and your daughters. You would make a stand for their sake.'

The Major sighed, and the flush faded from his thin cheeks.

' I could once,' he said in the old despairing voice. ' I had the strength once to resist the devil—it is a real devil, a roaring devil going about seeking whom he may devour, and he has devoured me !—but I have no strength left now to resist him. Ah! young man, you don't know what it is to be old and worn out, and too feeble to help yourself.'

' That is just the time to go to the Great Helper and put one's self in His hands. You will never be able to keep this pledge in your own strength——'

' No, no, no !' interrupted the Major almost fiercely. ' I tell you I have no fight left in me. I will sign whatever you like, but I warn you that nothing can keep me when—when——'

'We won't talk about that,' said Stephen. 'We'll just ask Him who has said that there shall no temptation happen to man stronger than he can bear, that with the temptation, with *this* temptation, there shall be a way of escape.'

Then Stephen knelt down beside the table, with the fair unsullied pages of the pledge-book open before him, and asked God to keep his weak, erring servant from falling, to strengthen him in his hour of temptation, to raise him up out of the mire and slough of moral degradation into which he had fallen, and to beat down Satan under his feet. It was a great deal to ask.

While he asked it the unhappy man slipped off the chair on which he was sitting, and knelt down before the grate, with its

white ashes and dying embers ; and, kneeling on the hearth he had outraged, he raised
his feeble hands to Heaven, and solemnly
pledged himself, with God's help, to resist
the Devil, and wrestle with all the strength
that God had given him against princi-
palities and powers, against the awful, unutterable legion that Satan might bring
against him, and in that dread hour, Stephen
Dashwood, kneeling by his side, prayed that
he should not be left alone.

'Give me the pen,' he said eagerly, when
he got up from his knees—'give me the
pen !'

Stephen gave him the pen, and he signed
his name, the honourable name he had
dragged in the dust :

Augustus Drummond Grove.

He wrote it in full, a long, nervous, aristo-
cratic signature—a signature of which every

letter was so shaky and irregular that it was impossible to recognise it. A spider released from an inkpot, trailing over the page, might have produced a similar result.

He threw the pen down, and dropped wearily into his chair, and let his face fall into his hands in the old manner.

Stephen, seeing that he desired to be alone, went out, carrying the book with him. Before he went he laid his hand gently on the Major's shoulder and bent over him.

'God bless you,' he said, in a voice that he could not keep quite steady, 'and give you strength to keep the pledge you have taken! Remember, "To him that over-cometh——"'

Major Grove slipped his shoulder from under Stephen's hand.

'Yes, yes,' he said impatiently; 'but what to him that is overcome?'

Stephen sighed as he closed the door; it

wasn't very encouraging, though he had his
signature, such as it was, in the shabby book
under his arm.   He hadn't much faith in him.

Doll was waiting for him in the passage
outside ; she had been walking up and down
the passage all the time, and most likely
she had heard every word that had been
spoken behind that closed door.

She had had time, while Stephen had
gone to the Rectory to fetch the book, to
look in the glass.   She was always ready to
look in the glass ; she ought to have known
pretty well by this time the image she saw
reflected there, but to-day what she saw there
startled her.   It showed her what she would
be some day, what sorrow and suffering
might make her any day.

It was a dreadful revelation ; she had to
look twice to be sure it was her own dis-
ordered image that the unsympathizing glass
gave back.

She had found time to bathe her eyes, and gather up her beautiful hair ; she would have given it a twist with the tongs, but Mary was calling her. She looked more like the old Doll when Stephen came back, but her face was hard, and there were two red spots burning on her white cheeks.

'Well,' she said, when the door had closed behind him ; ' has he signed it ?'

' Yes,' Stephen said, as cheerfully as he could—' oh yes, he has signed the pledge.'

' How long will he keep it ?' Doll said scornfully, with a hard glitter in her eyes. ' Oh, I have no patience with him ! He has only done this because he is frightened. When—when it is over he will break out again. He will kill Mary-gold or me, most likely.'

' I trust not,' Stephen said sadly ; ' there is nothing else, I'm afraid, to be done —not —not at present. We can only pray for him. You must ask God to give him strength to keep the promise he has made. You and your sister, you must both pray for him. You must ask in faith.'

Doll's thin lips curled.

' I am afraid our prayers will not be much good to him,' she said dryly. ' Mother and Mary-gold haven't ceased praying for him for years and years, and they don't seem to have done him any good.'

' We don't know,' Stephen said sadly. ' Prayer is often answered in a way we least expect ; we are sure only of one thing, that God hears it, and in His own time and His own way He will answer it.'

He went sadly down the steps of the chill, darkened house, into the sweet summer sun-shine. A weight was on his heart, and there was a mist before his eyes. He hadn't much faith in Major Grove.

' What else could he do ?' he asked him-

self all the way back to the Rectory, and
he hadn't answered the question when he
reached the gate.

The work was not his, he told himself ;
it was his Master's. If there was to be
a miracle, He alone could work it. If the
tiny seed of repentance was ever to wake
to life, the Divine Husbandman alone could
awake it ; and this late awakening would be
the beginning of miracles.

.

END OF VOL. I.

BILLING AND SONS, PRINTERS, GUILDFORD.